DRAGONS OF BOURBON SREET

JADE CALHOUN SERIES, BOOK 9

DEANNA CHASE

ABOUT THIS BOOK

White witch Jade Calhoun is seven months pregnant. All she wants to do is sink into domestic bliss while enjoying planning wedding and baby showers. But when a new acquaintance is arrested by the Witches Council and then mysteriously disappears, Jade is pulled into the thick of things. Forced by the Witches Council to track down the missing woman, Jade finds herself once again dealing with dragons.

It should be a piece of cake, right? All she needs to do is track down the woman who escaped the Council, stop the dragons from awakening and taking over the city, and still find time to celebrate life's milestones... all while in her third trimester.

CHAPTER 1

"*J*ade, this would look hot on you." Pyper held up a sexy little black lace number with matching panties against her white tank top and short electric-blue skirt. She'd finished the outfit with strappy white flats that showed off her electric-blue toenails. "It's classy, and with your amazing new boobs spilling out of the bodice, Kane will lose his mind."

I glanced down and placed my hands over my protruding belly as I scoffed. "Have you lost your mind? I passed my sexy phase two or three months ago. Trust me. There is nothing about this seven-month-pregnant body that screams seduction."

Pyper stepped back, still holding the scraps of fabric in her hands, and shook her head as she eyed me. "Girl, you look so good that even those guys over there in the corner stopped searching for porn to gawk at you. Look, the blond one is practically drooling."

My face heated as I followed her gaze to the two men in the corner of the adult novelty store. We'd stopped into Hustler Hollywood to pick up a few things for our friend Kat's bachelorette party and had somehow moved on to shopping for Pyper. She was looking for baby-making outfits for her next date night with her fiancé Julius.

"Pyper," I said with an uncomfortable laugh. "They're in the pregnancy-fetish porn aisle. Of course they're staring at me."

"Oops. You're right." Pyper grimaced and raised her arm, waving at the two men who were still leering. As they started to make their way over, she held her hand up. "That's close enough, pervs. My friend here is married and not interested in being your fantasy of the week. Eyes back on the porno movies, got it?"

"No can do," the blond one said, lust streaming off him and making my skin crawl as it crept over my bare arms. Being an empath sucked when you were forced to deal with a horny SOB with a pregnancy fetish. "Your friend is the hottest thing I've seen since *Plugging*—"

"Stop right there unless you want my friend to curse your manhood into a shriveled relic of rotted wood," Pyper said with a saccharine smile.

"Curse?" He threw his head back and laughed. "Sure, babe. Whatever you say."

The two of them continued to guffaw about Pyper's threat. I just rolled my eyes. The chances of me cursing someone's man bits were pretty small, but if they stepped out of line, I wouldn't hesitate to put them in their place.

"Okay, so about this black lingerie," Pyper said with a grin. "If you don't get it, I'm buying it for you as a present for Kane. I happen to know he still thinks you're sexy as hell."

There was no doubt she would. "If you do and I look like a beached whale, don't be surprised when something smaller and dirtier shows up when your pregnant belly is hanging over your elastic jeans so far that you can't see your feet any longer."

Pyper's eyes gleamed. "I have a feeling you'll have trouble finding something I don't already own."

All I could do was laugh at her. Wasn't she going to be surprised when her entire body ached from being swollen and her bladder was complaining all the time? Sexy time might've been mind-blowing a few months ago, but lately... Well, as much as I loved Kane's attention, sleep was number one on my list of recreational activities. "We'll see."

"What do you think of this?" She held up a strappy leather thing that looked like it would require instructions to figure out how to wear it.

"I think it's probably a little wild for Julius," I said with a shrug. "He seems more like a silk kind of guy."

She nodded and put the contraption back on the rack. "You're probably right about that, though he's never been too picky when it comes to my seduction techniques."

I snorted and selected a silver lace corset and matching garter set from the rack. "None of them are. Here, try this."

Her eyes lit up. "That's perfect. He'll love it."

"Good. Let's take care of the items on the list for Kat's

party now." I handed her the bustier and noted she was still clutching the lace number she'd threatened to buy for Kane. Resigned that I was going to end up with it one way or another, I held my hand out. "Give it here. Kane can pay for it."

"He's going to thank me later." She winked, handed me the garments, and moved on to eye the penis headbands.

"Definitely get those," I said as I grabbed a jar of edible Honey Dust and chocolate body paint.

"Someone has plans." Pyper grinned as she made her way down an aisle to inspect something that looked suspiciously like nipple clamps.

"Please. They're for Kat's wedding shower. I was— Hey!" The glee hit me square in the back like an arrow plunging into my skin just before a pair of hands landed on my ass. I spun around as I backed up, putting distance between my groper and myself. "What the hell do you think you're doing?"

The blond guy who'd been searching pregnancy porn gave me a cocky grin and raised his hands palms up as he said, "That ass, it was just right there. What else was I supposed to do?"

"Hey, asshole!" Pyper snarled, hurrying back toward us. "What did I say about leaving my friend alone?"

Still shocked he'd just blatantly grabbed my ass, I stood there blinking in disbelief. Had that really just happened? But then he reached out, his hands heading for my belly as his lust started to prickle my skin again. Oh, hell no.

"Don't even think about it," I said through clenched teeth, magic already sparking at my fingertips.

"I just want to feel your… *bump*," he said, his tone seriously creepy.

I tried to back up but ran right into a display of edible panties, causing the product pyramid to crash to the floor, and still the man kept coming. Time seemed to slow down, and I felt frozen in disgust as his hands inched toward me.

He let out a small moan as his fingers lightly brushed over the barely exposed skin between my tank top and stretchy yoga pants.

I snapped out of my horrified trance, and my magic flew straight for his crotch. The white stream of power lit him up like a firecracker as he flew backward, his hands covering his electrified privates. He tripped over his own feet and sprawled to the floor, his mouth open in a shocked *O* and terror in his wide, dilated eyes.

Great. He was high on something. I stalked across the store and stared down at him, my hands still sparking with electric magic. I held them out so he could see just how dangerous I could still be. "Do anything like that again, and I'll blow it right off. Got it?"

"It's already gone, you crazy bitch!" he cried, clutching his crotch.

His anger swirled around him like a red haze, but my own rage-induced magic was keeping it from affecting me in any way. Good. Otherwise it would drain me, and my afternoon nap would likely turn into a sixteen-hour sleeping marathon.

His lips twisted into a snarl. "You turned it into a shriveled, burned piece of wood!"

"Not yet, but I will," I growled back.

"Yeah!" Pyper chimed in, pressing her boot to his side. "And when she's done, I'll crack a rib or two."

"Back off!" Pervy's friend cried, trying to come to his rescue. "All he did was cop a feel. He doesn't deserve to have his dick blown off."

"No?" I said, my rage making my entire body shake. "I beg to differ. Better get your jackass friend out of here before I call the police and file an assault charge."

"You assaulted me!" Pervy whimpered as his friend hauled him to his feet.

A short redheaded woman ran over, a small fluffy dog at her heels. "I'm so sorry, Ms. Calhoun. Vic is on his way downstairs to escort this man out of the store."

"No!" Pervy shook off his friend, panic taking over as his gaze darted for the stairs. "I'm going."

Loud footsteps sounded on the wooden stairs in the back of the store.

The pair hurried to the front door.

"Don't come back... ever," the redhead called after them.

"I spend hundreds here every month!" he spat out as he hesitated at the door.

"More like tens," she said dryly and gave him a flat stare.

"Bitch," he snarled.

She shrugged. "If the shoe fits."

Clearly pissed he hadn't ruffled her feathers, he whirled and stormed out.

The clerk turned to me and lifted one shoulder. "I don't think he likes me much."

Pyper laughed and shook her head, amused. "I think we're going to be good friends."

I grinned at the sales clerk. "Same." Holding my hand out, I asked, "You seem to know me, but I don't think we've met."

She beamed and shook my hand with both of hers. "I'm Harper Spelling. We haven't actually met yet, but you're sort of famous in my circle."

"Famous?" I asked just as the baby kicked one of my ribs. "Oomph. That was a good one. She gets a little excited when I use my magic."

Pyper sobered and eyed me. "Everything all right? Do I need to take you to the healer?"

I rolled my eyes. "No. You're just as bad as Kane is these days. I'm fine. The baby's fine. And that jackass who groped me is gonna be out of commission for a week or so while he recovers from the swift bolt of magic to his nuts. Everything's good."

"Man, I really wish I had that skill. Magic to the crotch would be preferable to straining a muscle during a physical altercation," Pyper said wistfully.

"I couldn't agree more," Harper said and turned her attention to the large man who'd finally made his way onto the bottom floor of the store. He was tall, close to seven feet, with bulging muscles, and he had a scowl on his face fit for a WWF wrestler ready to rip an opponent's head off. "We're good, Vic. Just the idea of dealing with you sent the jackass running."

"Perfect." He smiled at her, his entire face softening and making him look like a giant teddy bear. "My reputation is finally paying off." The man winked at us and strode back toward the stairs.

"He's... Wow," I said, admiring the man's ability to portray two completely different personas.

"Definitely wow. And handsome too," Pyper said. "If I wasn't already spoken for, it'd be hard to keep me from following him upstairs."

"Yeah," Harper said with a wistful sigh. "He's yummy."

I chuckled softly, watching Harper and Pyper barely hold back the drool as they stared at Vic's backside until he disappeared to the second floor. He was definitely hot in a pure-testosterone sort of way. But in my view, no one held a candle to Kane... not even a Jason Momoa look-alike with muscles to match.

"So, Harper," I said, clearing my throat. "You said I was famous in your circle. I can't imagine what circle that would be unless you're a witch. And if you are, you should certainly check out the New Orleans coven."

"Oh no, definitely not a witch," she said, lowering her voice and glancing around the showroom as if looking to see who might be listening. "Though I have a second cousin who is. She's been living in Salem the past couple of years."

"That's pretty on the nose," I said with a laugh. "Does she wear black and a pointed witch hat and run a novelty witchcraft store?"

Harper burst out laughing. "Yes, as a matter of fact, she does." Her smile was radiant, and her eyes sparkled with joy. "It's a total tourist trap where she sells mostly fake wands and harmless love spells. But she enjoys it, so who am I to judge?"

Pride radiated from the woman in the form of bright white light that only I could see.

"I'm friends with Mati Ballentine," Harper continued. "We go to school together at Tulane, and I happened to be in the Pointe that day when y'all brought down that dragon. It was crazy and awe-inspiring the way you saved the city from the dragon and yet still rescued Conor." She bowed slightly at the waist and mimed tipping an imaginary hat. "So impressive."

She was referring to the incident a few months ago when the actor Conor Wells had been possessed by a dragon's soul and had actually turned into a full-fledged flying dragon. With the help of the Coven Pointe witches, I'd been able to capture him so that the angel council could force the dragon soul out of his body and back into a statue where it had been previously contained for hundreds of years. Conor was back to his normal self, once again working on his hit television show *Witchin' Hills*, and the dragon soul was safe in the angel realm.

I gave her a tight smile, uncomfortable to be talking about a major breach in the paranormal world right there in the middle of the store. "Thanks. I had some help."

"I was wondering if we could get together and talk sometime soon… in private? There's something brewing here in New Orleans, and I think—" The store phone started to ring, and she grimaced, holding up one finger. "Hold that thought. I have to get that."

"Sure," I said, curiosity rolling through me as she hurried through the aisles of penis pops and edible undies to grab the phone. The knowledge that there was something, likely a paranormal something, going on in New Orleans wasn't surprising. New Orleans was a hotbed of paranormal shenanigans, but it would be a nice change to be forewarned for once.

"Come on," Pyper said. "Let's finish up and get out of here."

I nodded and followed her around the store as we gathered enough supplies to open our own mini store. If Kat didn't have a good time at both her bachelorette party and wedding shower, it wasn't going to be for a lack of trying.

As Harper finished ringing us up at the register, I asked, "What was that you were saying earlier before you were interrupted by the phone? Something about a problem brewing here in New Orleans?"

She nodded and frowned as she opened her mouth to speak, but before she could get the words out, the door swung open and three witches I recognized strode in. Madam Tempest, the leader of the Witches' Council, was flanked by two other council witches, a white-haired male and a pretty brunette. I'd had the unfortunate experience of being on trial in front of them a few months ago after the Conor / dragon fiasco. I'd been accused of a variety of things, including breaking and entering and endangering the citizens of New Orleans.

"Madam Tempest—" I started, but the witch wasn't paying any attention to me.

Instead, she held her hand out toward Harper and said, "Bind she who seeks to unleash the dragon."

Tendrils of braided light shot from her fingertips and encircled Harper's wrists, locking them together.

"Hey!" Harper cried, her eyes wide and fear seeping off her in the form of a stinky green gas that made my stomach roll from the noxious fumes. "I didn't do any—" Her words were cut off as the magical light shot to her lips, magically sealing them together. She thrashed her head back and forth as she murmured, "Mmmm mmm."

"What is going on?" I forced out as I wiped my watering eyes. "Madam Tempest, what do you mean, 'unleash the dragon'?"

The leader of the Witches' Council turned her head, finally acknowledging my presence. "Jade Calhoun," she said flatly. "I would've thought you'd have enough good sense to stay away from the dragon business after the incident earlier this summer."

"I don't have any idea what you're talking about," I said indignantly. "Did the dragon escape again?"

"No." She snapped her fingers, and Harper moved from behind the counter, her limbs jerky. It was obvious the young woman was being forced against her will as Madam Tempest pointed at her and then the door, causing Harper to march outside.

Madam Tempest and her minions followed. The second the three of them stepped onto the sidewalk, the foursome disappeared into the ether.

"Holy shit," Pyper said, her eyes wide as she stared at the empty sidewalk.

"You can say that again."

A small bark sounded from behind us as the chocolate-colored puppy with velvet-textured fur darted out from behind the counter. The little dog skidded to a stop in front of the door, growled, and then opened her mouth and let out a roar of pure fire.

CHAPTER 2

*P*yper blinked, her eyes wide. "What the hell just happened?"

We both stared at the small animal who stood in the middle of the store, smoke seeping out of her nostrils.

"I don't know, but what is *that*?" I asked in a whisper, not at all sure the creature couldn't understand me. It looked like a miniature schnauzer, but if it could breathe fire, who knew what it actually was or what else it could do?

The imposter dog trotted over to me and rubbed her head against my leg.

"Looks like a fire-breathing puppy to me," Pyper said.

I gave her a flat stare. "Thanks, captain obvious."

She shrugged one shoulder. "I do what I can."

"What is that smell!" Vic shouted as he stormed down the stairs.

Pyper and I grimaced at each other. In the excitement,

I'd forgotten that Vic was even in the store. His boots hit the wood floors, the sound echoing through the building.

His eyes were bulging and his face red as he came to a stop a few feet from us and roared, "Who lit the door on fire?"

My gaze landed on the door in question. It wasn't actually on fire; it was just charred a little. The fire-breathing dog scooted to hide behind me. I couldn't say I blamed her. Vic was pissed.

"A few witches from the council were here. They arrested Harper," I said, ignoring his question.

"Witches' Council? Harper's a witch?" His brow furrowed in confusion.

"I don't think so. She said she wasn't." All I knew was that she had something to do with dragons, which were a major sore spot with the council. I glanced down at the fire-breathing beast and wondered if she was going to turn into a winged creature at any moment. I reached down and scooped her up.

"What are you doing?" Pyper whispered, eyeing the dog with wariness.

"We can't leave her here," I said.

The chocolate-colored ball of fur curled into my arms and pressed her little face against my chest. But as I patted her head, she let out a small burp, followed by a burst of fire. Intense heat blew by my arm, the fire barely missing me.

"Whoa!" I jerked my body back and held her away from me. "Careful. You're gonna hurt someone that way."

She gave me a sheepish look and tucked her muzzle into her body as she started to shake.

"Goddess above, I think she's scared," I said to Pyper, snuggling her against my chest again.

"Scared!" Vic yelled. "That thing did this to the door, didn't it? I knew there was something wrong with that dog the minute Harper brought her in here. No puppy is that well behaved. I knew it had to be possessed." Vic grabbed the phone and sent us a disgusted glare. "You should let animal control take it before it burns your face off."

"She's not possessed," I said, hoping I was speaking the truth. But she very well could be, and that was a strong reason for not turning her over to a mundane city authority. Fear and anxiety were clinging to the dog, making her shake slightly. And that more than anything was what convinced me to take her home. Usually I couldn't sense an animal's emotional energy, so that likely meant the dog wasn't really a dog. Maybe a familiar.

"We'll take her to a shelter," Pyper said.

What? I mouthed. No freaking way were we dropping her off at some random shelter.

Pyper sent me a *shut up* look. Then she said, "And we'll find out why the Witches' Council arrested Harper."

"Don't bother. The manager is going to have a shit-fit when he sees this destruction." Vic grumbled as he punched numbers on the phone. "You'll want to have that beast far from here when he arrives, otherwise it won't be pretty."

I tightened my hold on the dog. "What does that mean?"

"It means that dog isn't long for this world if Zeph gets his hands on it." Vic turned his back to us, pressed the

15

phone to his ear, and said, "Zeph? It's Vic. We have a problem."

"We better go," I said to Pyper, concerned for both the dog and Harper.

She grabbed our packages from the counter and nodded. "I'm right behind you."

"WE NEED to get in touch with Mati," I said, pulling a half-eaten cheesecake out of my fridge. We were back at the house I shared with Kane in the French Quarter and had congregated in the kitchen at the back of the shotgun double. "If Harper really is friends with her, Mati might have some clue what Madam Tempest meant when she said Harper was trying to unleash dragons. She also might know what Harper was talking about when she said something was brewing in New Orleans."

"And Bea and Lailah," Pyper added and took a sip of coffee. "If it has to do with dragons, they'll need to know."

I eyed her mug wistfully and did a mental calculation of how long it would be before I could partake in the glorious caffeine-filled beverage. "I think we should find out what we're up against before we call in the cavalry. Besides, if Harper's really messing with dragons, maybe there's nothing to worry about. Maybe the council is already on top of things."

Pyper raised both eyebrows. "You don't really believe that though, do you? They didn't exactly handle the Conor thing very well."

"I honestly don't know." I sliced off a piece of cheesecake and took a bite before I added, "You're right. They completely botched the Conor thing, and there seemed to be a lot of politicking going on. But Bea doesn't have the best relationship with them, and Lailah is busy dealing with angel stuff up in the angel realm. I think I just want to get a handle on what's happening before we bother them. We don't even know anything yet."

"I could call Julius, see if he's heard anything," Pyper offered. Her fiancé worked for the council, but his cases were much more low profile than one that might involve dragons.

"You can try," I said. "Doubtful he knows anything."

She nodded her agreement, then stared me in the eye as she asked, "Are you sure you don't want to call Bea? Her connections are unparalleled."

"I'm sure." Bea had retired from the coven some months back, and I hated bringing every unusual thing right to her doorstep. She'd retired for a reason. Besides, she'd helped me research and understand dragon lore a few months back, and it was clear she'd shared all her dragon knowledge with me then. I'd be shocked if she knew anything about unleashing dragons, whatever that meant.

"And what about that little ball of joy?" Pyper asked, pointing to the schnauzer.

The dog was lying flat on her belly, nose to nose with Duke, my golden retriever ghost dog. The schnauzer might have been a fire-breathing beast, but Duke seemed to like her and that was good enough for me.

"She can stay here with us for the time being."

Pyper gave me a look. "What if she burps and burns your eyebrows off?"

I chuckled. "I'll just have to keep my distance. That creature isn't a dog, and in the hands of the mundane, she'd be in serious danger."

"And so would they. You're probably right to keep her. So, first plan of action?"

"Head to Coven Pointe and find Mati. Want to join me?" I put the cheesecake back in the fridge and grabbed the leftover mac and cheese.

"Uh, yes. You don't think I'm letting you go by yourself, do you?" she asked, her tone incredulous.

I laughed. "I'm just going to talk to a friend, Pyper. Not break Harper out of the witch jail."

"Yeah, sure." One eyebrow was raised as she studied me. "And when she tells you Harper is just an innocent college girl, what then? Are you just going to leave her in the Witches' Council's hands, or are you going to storm the castle so to speak and demand she be released?"

I shrugged. She was right of course. If I was certain Harper was innocent and the council had overstepped, I couldn't do nothing. I'd probably demand her release. But what I'd do after that remained to be seen. "You wouldn't let her sit in jail and do nothing either."

"I'm not seven months pregnant."

"But you have a brother you're responsible for and a fiancé," I countered as I put the mac and cheese in the microwave. "Can we just wait until we know something before we have this fight?"

"What fight?" Kane said, appearing out of thin air. His

dark hair was slightly mussed, and to my eyes he was sexy as hell in his low-slung jeans and tight white T-shirt.

Pyper jumped and placed a hand on her heart. "Holy hell! I swear, we need to put a bell on you. You should warn a person before you do that," she said to him, frowning.

Kane was an incubus and a member of the Brotherhood, an organization that kept the city safe from demons. He was also a Shadow Walker, which meant he could walk between worlds and slip into the shadows at one location and slip out in another, rendering transportation somewhat unnecessary. I was used to him popping in and out. Pyper clearly wasn't.

I gave my husband a warm smile and practically floated into his arms. He bent and kissed the top of my head and used one hand to knead the muscles at the base of my neck. I let out a small groan of pleasure. "That feels amazing."

His chocolate eyes flashed instantly with pure need as he gazed down at me in appreciation. "That sound, Jade... You're killing me."

My entire body tingled with his desire as it washed over me, making my skin heat. His incubus nature was in full force, lighting me up like a firecracker. I tried to take a step back, put a bit of distance between us, but he held on, keeping me pressed against his muscular body.

"My god, you two. I'm sitting right here," Pyper said. "Try to remember that as you're mentally undressing each other."

I laughed, my face heating slightly from embarrassment. "Maybe that little black number really will get put to use."

"Little black number?" Kane asked, his fingers caressing my neck again, sending shivers down my spine.

"You'll thank me later." Pyper pumped her eyebrows.

"Sounds like it," he said, his eyes twinkling. "But just in case I forget, thank you. My libido will be forever grateful for your thoughtfulness."

"Your libido doesn't need any help," I said, fanning myself. Then the microwave beeped, and I stepped away to grab my lunch as I added, "Hey. You're home early. Does that mean the demon-hunting business is slow today, or are you just regrouping before you and the guys head out for another hunt?"

"Just home early. Apparently it's too hot even for demons." He winked and reached past me to grab a beer out of the fridge. Glancing back at Pyper, he asked, "Want one?"

"Yes." She gave him a decisive nod and leaned back in her chair.

I eyed the Guinness bottles wistfully and sighed as Kane handed me a sparkling water.

"Just a few more months, shortcake," he said with a warm smile.

I pressed my hands to my belly and felt the familiar peace I always experienced when I focused on our daughter. "It's fine. I wouldn't trade this moment for the world."

His eyes softened as he watched me and then let his gaze fall to my belly. "Me neither."

Pyper let out an audible sigh. "You guys... Dammit. Now you're making me teary. You know how much I hate that."

Kane sat down at the table across from Pyper. "Do you want to hear about the demon we sent back to hell today?

He had warts covering his face and spikes sticking out of his ears."

"Gross," she said, shaking her head. "That's quite enough."

"Okay then." He took a long swig of his beer, and when he set the bottle down with a thunk, he said, "So, what's this I hear about my two favorite girls having a fight?"

"We're not fighting." I took a seat next to him. After forking a bite of macaroni and cheese, I said, "Not yet anyway."

"Yes, we are." Pyper picked at the edge of the label on her beer bottle. "She's ready to step right into the middle of something that has to do with dragons and the Witches' Council... again. And I think she should probably stay out of this one."

I glared at her, tired of being treated like a fragile piece of glass. "Listen. I appreciate the concern, but I'm not going to break. If anything, now that I have the baby on board, I'm more powerful than ever. Besides, so far all we know is that Harper was arrested. We have no idea if she was into anything dangerous. I think you're overreacting just a little."

"I think someone needs to fill me in," Kane said, glancing between us.

At that moment, the little brown schnauzer ran out from behind the kitchen island, barking like a crazy dog as if she'd just realized Kane had arrived. She skidded to a stop at his feet, sniffed his leg, then started to growl.

"Who might this be?" he asked me, both eyebrows raised.

"Harper's... uh, dog?" I said with a small grimace.

"You say that like you're not sure. It definitely looks like a dog to me." He glanced down at the puppy, who was still growling but had backed up and was now pressing herself against my leg.

"She has some interesting abilities." I took a moment to fill him in on the details of the afternoon, including the charring of the store's door.

"This thing breathes fire?" he asked, peering at the dog.

"She's not a thing," I said defensively. "She's just a fire-breathing puppy. Maybe a familiar."

"Or a demon," he said, reaching for her.

Just as his hand went around her middle, she let out a yelp, jumped out of his reach, and let loose another round of fire, charring the leg of the table.

"Jesus!" Kane jerked his hands back and slid his chair a few feet away from her. "That dragon-dog is dangerous. Jade, we can't have her here. She'll burn the place to the ground."

I reached down, waited for the puppy to come to me, and then lifted her into my lap. She was shaking again, and prickles of her fear coated my hands. "No, she definitely isn't a demon." My tone left no room for debate. "And she's only breathing fire because she's frightened. I can feel her emotions. They're a little more muted than a human's, but I can definitely feel them." I met Kane's eyes, silently pleading. "I can't take her to a shelter. They won't know what to do with her. I'll take her to Mati's. She's friends with Harper. Maybe she can watch her until this thing with Harper is resolved."

He sighed heavily. "Jade... if she can't, you're going to bring her back here, aren't you?"

I gave him a bright smile. "You would too if you'd saved her from being sent to the pound."

"I doubt it," he mumbled and shook his head, but I knew in that moment I'd won that round. As much as he wasn't into a fire-breathing dragon-dog, he was a big softie when it came to animals. He'd do the same thing if the choice was left to him.

I put the puppy on the floor and moved to stand next to my husband. After draping an arm over his shoulders, I leaned down and kissed him on the cheek. "Thank you."

He snaked his arm around my hips and rested his hand on my lower belly. "Pyper has a point. The last thing we need right now is you getting into it with the Witches' Council. And if Harper really is messing with dragons, then maybe they were right to take her. After what happened with Conor, I can't say I'm crazy about another one flying over the city of New Orleans anytime soon."

"Don't worry. I'm not in any hurry to tangle with a dragon or land in jail again," I said, knowing he was less concerned about my using magic and how it might affect our baby than he was about what the Witches' Council would do if I got in their way. They weren't exactly a forgiving group. When it came to their laws, there weren't any shades of gray. "I just want to talk to Mati and make sure this girl has someone on her side. The council..." I frowned and shook my head. "They tend to imprison first and ask questions later."

"Can't argue with that," Kane said. "Want me to come with?"

"Do you want to? Or would you prefer prepping a

bedroom picnic for later? That little black number is sounding better and better all the time," I said, imagining him running his hands softly over every inch of my bare skin. Earlier an intimate encounter with Kane hadn't been on my radar, but now that his incubus energy had infiltrated my defenses, I was fully on board. Pregnancy or not, I wanted him, all of him, and soon.

"Bedroom picnic. For sure," he said and mouthed a thank-you toward Pyper.

"You're welcome," she said. "Just remember this when you're out with Julius and the opportunity to step into a lingerie store comes up. The answer is always yes, and make him get me something scandalous, okay?"

"Got it." He raised his beer and they clinked the bottles together, both wearing sly, mischievous smiles.

Goddess above. They were so much alike—it was no wonder they were best friends.

Forking another bite of mac and cheese, I glanced at Pyper. "Just give me ten minutes to wolf down this food and then we can get going."

She snorted. "More like three. I've seen you eat."

"Ha ha," I said dryly. But three minutes later, I'd already dumped my bowl in the sink, texted Mati to let her know we were on our way, and scooped up the dragon-dog. "Let's do this."

She drained the last of her beer and then followed me out the front door.

CHAPTER 3

"I've always loved this car," Pyper said as she stepped on the gas pedal and whipped through the French Quarter. "And I gave Kane so much shit when he bought it."

"Why?" I stroked the puppy's ears, trying to keep her calm. She was curled up on my baby bump, pressing her head against me. We'd tried securing her in the back with the seat belt, but she wasn't having any of it. The smoke had started almost instantly, and I decided it was better to hold her than let her burn the Lexus from the inside out.

"Because it just screams rich asshole." She laughed. "He didn't take kindly to that comment."

"I'd imagine not." Kane had inherited his grandmother's house in the French Quarter and another plantation house outside of town. Those two properties had afforded him the ability to build up a couple of businesses, which meant he was more than comfortable. He'd even helped Pyper open the Grind, her coffee shop on Bourbon Street. Rich he might be, but asshole he wasn't.

"You know I can't resist needling him." She steered the car onto the Crescent City Connection bridge that would take us over the river and to Coven Pointe. "Before Bo came along, he was the closest thing I had to a brother."

"How is Bo?" I asked, inquiring after the teenager she'd met less than a year ago. After she realized they shared the same deadbeat father who'd up and left Bo with a jackass who only cared about a foster care check from the state, she'd brought him home and become his legal guardian.

"Good. He and Reagan are working full time at the Grind for now. Once school starts up again, I'll need to find someone else to fill in for you." She eyed my belly. "I suppose making lattes is off the table for a while."

I'd been working at her café since the first month I'd stumbled into New Orleans. The truth was, I loved working with her, but now that I had a baby on board, I was taking an extended leave of absence. "Yes, but if you need help, you can always call. I'm sure the peanut can ride along in a mommy sling."

She waved an unconcerned hand. "We'll find someone."

Pyper maneuvered through the city streets, avoiding the potholes with expert precision, and finally came to a stop right outside Mati's raised-basement home. Before I even managed to get my seat belt off, Pyper was on the sidewalk, holding my door open and reaching for the dog.

The pup grunted and once again snorted smoke.

"You're trouble, you know that?" Pyper asked her as she frowned at the small creature. "You need a name."

"How about Flame?" I offered as I hauled myself out of the seat, pleased I'd made it upright without help.

"If the shoe fits," Pyper said, handing me the dog. "Flame it is."

Still holding Flame, I followed Pyper up the stairs to Mati's apartment. Before she could even knock, the door flew open and Mati beamed at us. Her dark hair was piled up on her head in a haphazard bun, but the tendrils were curled, giving her a slightly mussed but gorgeous look.

"Pyper! Jade! It's been such a long time. Come in." She held the door open and waved us in. "And who's this little cutie?" She reached for Flame, but I held her back.

"She belongs to Harper, and she has... unusual abilities," I said.

"Harper?" Mati asked, surprise in her tone as she tucked one of those tendrils behind her ear. "Since when? As far as I know, she doesn't have any power at all. Just an interest in the supernatural. She believes in the power of energy but can't actually feel it like you can, Jade."

Interesting. No wonder she'd done her homework on who I was. Being that I was an empath, energy was pretty much my thing.

"No. This one." I pointed to the dog. "She breathes fire."

Mati's eyes went wide then narrowed as she studied Flame. "That's not a dog, is it?"

Pyper and I shared a glance and I shook my head. "I don't think so. I'm guessing a familiar."

"Oh man." Mati pressed a hand to her forehead. "This is bad. Really bad. Do you know where Harper is? There's a message on my voice mail from this morning, but when I tried to call her back, the guy who answered the phone told me she didn't work there anymore."

"She called you?" I asked. "When?"

"While I was in class this morning. I found the message on my phone about an hour ago. Why?"

"Maybe we should sit down while we talk," I said, eyeing the overstuffed leather couch against the wall.

"Sure." Mati waved a hand, inviting us to take a seat. Vaughn, another member of the Brotherhood, walked in wearing ripped jeans, a formfitting T-shirt, and white athletic shoes. His dark hair was still wet from a shower, and I couldn't help thinking that besides Kane, he was just about the most handsome man I'd ever met. He stood next to Mati, and the pair of them were so beautiful together they looked like they'd just walked right off the pages of *Cosmopolitan* magazine.

Mati smiled up at him. "Hey there. Can you get us some tea?" Her head swiveled to me. "Do you need anything else? A snack? Cookies? Crackers?"

"Jade always needs cookies," Pyper said with a teasing smile. "Me too for that matter, and I don't even have an excuse." She patted her flat stomach.

"Cookies it is," Vaughn said.

"Water for me," I said. "No caffeine while the baby's on board."

"Right." Vaughn kissed Mati on the cheek before disappearing into the kitchen.

"He's..." Pyper shook her head and fanned herself.

"That's an incubus for you," Mati said with an amused smile. "He even manages to turn the heads of the happily committed."

I laughed. She wasn't kidding. Pyper and I were completely off the market with no desire to stray... ever, and yet we'd both been dazzled by Vaughn. I swear, someone needed to put a paper bag over the man's head just to save the female population of New Orleans from themselves.

"Okay," Mati said as she sank into a white armchair. "What's going on with Harper, and what made you come here?"

"She told me you were friends and she was here the day we took the dragon down," I said.

Mati nodded. "That's true. She's rushing the sorority Chessa made me join a while back."

My eyebrows shot straight up. "I thought you had to have magic to join."

"So did I," she said with a laugh. "But I guess there weren't enough of us, so they started letting in people who have a passion for the paranormal or are related to people with supernatural abilities." She shrugged. "Harper has a grandmother who was an angel and an aunt who was a witch. I don't think she has any abilities, but you never know with her history, right? Not to mention the fact that she has a fire-breathing dog. Regular folks don't usually end up with supernatural creatures."

That was true, and it made me wonder if there really was some power lying dormant deep down inside Harper.

"Listen." I scooted forward, leaning in as I spoke. "I'm not sure what's going on with her, but a few witches from the council showed up today at the store she works at and hauled her off."

"What?" She blinked and jerked back. "At the Hustler Hollywood store?"

"Yeah. Pyper and I were there to pick up a few things for a bachelorette party."

"And a few personal items," Pyper said with a smirk.

Mati snickered but then sobered as she glanced back at me. "Sorry. What do you mean they hauled her off? Why?"

"I don't know exactly," I said. "They said something about 'bind she who seeks to unleash the dragon.' And since she mentioned being here during the dragon fiasco a few months ago and she has a fire-breathing dog, I have to assume she's involved in something that deals with dragons. Do you know anything about it?"

Shock flittered over the young woman's face and she shook her head. "No. Harper? Dragons? I don't believe it." She looked at the dog that was curled around my feet and frowned. "But what about that one and the fact that she's been arrested? It doesn't look good for her, does it?"

I shook my head. "No. It doesn't."

Mati reached for her phone on the end table, tapped the screen a few times, and then turned up the volume as a message started to play. "Mati, it's Harper. I know you're in class right now, but I need you to call me as soon as you get this message. It's important. I think I'm… Well, let's just say there's something going down with some of the new recruits for Kappa Mu. They need our help. Call me."

"Something going down? What does that mean?" Pyper asked, her brow furrowed. "Like their fake IDs have been discovered and the party will be dry unless someone steps up, or something going down like a demon is on the loose and someone needs to send his ass back to hell type of thing?"

Mati raised both hands, palms up in an I-don't-know gesture. "Hard to say. She sounds worried but not panicked. I guess I need to get over to the house and find out if her message has anything to do with why the council arrested her, huh?"

"Probably a good idea," I said. "Do you want us to come with you?"

Mati glanced at my protruding belly and smiled as she shook her head. "Nah. Vaughn and I can handle it." She smiled up at him as he reentered the room and placed a tray of cookies and drinks on the coffee table. "We'll let you know what we find out."

"And Harper?" I asked. "Does she have someone on her side who can help her?" After my experience with the Witches' Council earlier in the year, I knew just how important it was to have representation at their kangaroo court. Even if Harper was guilty of dealing with dragons, she deserved someone to defend her, otherwise who knew what might happen to her.

"I'll talk to Dayla and see if she'll send the coven lawyer to help," Mati said, referring to her aunt who also happened to be Coven Pointe's coven leader. She grabbed a sugar cookie and waved a hand to us. "Eat up. They should still be warm."

Coven lawyer, I thought. Why didn't we have one of those? Lucien, my second-in-command of the coven and a skilled researcher, had defended me. But a lawyer would be handy to have around. I'd have to look into that. I eyed the cookies and practically drooled. When was the last time I'd eaten? Oh, right. Just before we'd come over I'd had mac and cheese and cheesecake. Goddess above, I was out of control. That didn't stop me from snagging two cookies though.

Pyper just shook her head at me as she took one for herself and sipped a cup of tea.

"There's one more thing," I said to Mati, gesturing to the small dog at my feet. "I didn't want to hand her over to animal control. Not with her ability anyway. It's too dangerous."

Mati nodded. "I can see that. Is she staying with you for the time being?"

I reached down and picked up the snuggly dog. She curled up on my baby bump again and pressed her head against my shoulder. I sighed. "I was going to let her, but Kane is uneasy about the fire-breathing thing. She already came very close to crispy-frying his hand earlier, accidentally, of course."

"Ouch," Mati said sympathetically.

"Right. Anyway, I was wondering if you knew anyone who could take care of her or if you were willing to do it since you're friends with Harper and all?" I knew I'd shot myself in the foot the moment I mentioned she'd almost given Kane a third-degree burn, but Mati deserved to know the truth. Besides, it hadn't sounded like Mati had actually even met the dog... familiar... whatever it was before I'd brought her over.

Mati grimaced. "I'm sorry, Jade. I'd love to help out, but my lease doesn't let me have pets."

"Right. Okay. It was worth a shot." I hoisted Flame into my arms, grabbed another cookie, and stood.

"I could ask around, see if anyone in the sorority is interested in dog-sitting, but most are renting and I—"

"It's okay," I said, quickly, letting her off the hook. "I figured it was a long shot."

Mati got to her feet as well and pet the puppy behind the ears. "What will you do with her now?"

I shrugged. "Take her back home, I guess. I can't give her to the shelter, so unless you know about a place that takes in magical pets, it looks like I'm stuck with her." The council would've previously been an option, but after my stay there, I just didn't feel like I could trust them. They didn't even feed me a decent meal despite my being pregnant and incarcerated for more than forty-eight hours. No. My maternal instincts were working overtime, and the pup was coming home with me.

"Kane is not going to be happy," Pyper said. "But if you treat him to that lacy black number, I'm guessing that might help smooth things over."

I laughed. She had a point. But lacy lingerie or not, I doubted Kane would fight me too hard on this issue. He wouldn't want to put the creature in danger either. Maybe I could train her to keep her fire-breathing in check. I turned to Mati. "Will you keep me up-to-date with Harper's case and if there's anything to worry about with your sorority recruits? Let me know if there's anything I can do?"

"Sure." Mati followed Pyper and me to her door.

"And if you hear anything more about dragons, give me a call, will you?" I gave an involuntary shudder, imagining a showdown of dragons and demons filling the streets of our gorgeous city. It would be complete destruction. Dragons had originally been the protectors of the angels against the demons. But back in the 1600s, there'd been an epic battle that had all but destroyed the city, and most of the dragons had been wiped out. At least one soul had survived, but he'd been contained in a dragon sculpture for hundreds of years before he'd managed to latch onto my magic and work his way into Conor Wells a few months back.

After Conor had turned into a full-fledged dragon he was captured, and the dragon soul had been forced out of him by the angels and was now contained in the angel realm. Conor was back to his old self, and as far as anyone knew, there weren't any more dragons just hanging out, waiting to be released. But if there was one thing I'd learned from being a witch in New Orleans... anything was possible.

"If you'll do the same," Mati said, walking out onto her porch with us.

"Not a problem," I said.

She reached over and scratched Flame behind the ear. "And take care of this cutie."

I smiled at her. "Definitely."

"And that little one in there." She nodded at my belly.

"Don't worry. We'll figure out what's going on with Harper and her friends. Your last couple of months of pregnancy should be worry free. We've got it from here."

I let out a chuckle, and as Pyper and I made our way back to Kane's car, I thought, *Famous last words.*

CHAPTER 4

"*M*ati jinxed us," Pyper said as she pulled the car over to the side of the road.

The blue and red lights were flashing from the front window of the nondescript black car behind us, and the sticky magic the witches had aimed at the Lexus, forcing it to slow, was starting to seep in through the windows.

My heart thumped against my chest, and my blood was rushing in my ears. What was going on? New Orleans didn't have a magical police force. Who were these witches? Magic sparked at my fingertips, my entire being on guard. "Are they government officials, do you think? Or are they just black witches causing trouble?"

Pyper glanced over her shoulder. "They are wearing robes. Official ones that look like they belong to the Witches' Council."

"Did Julius say anything about the council having law enforcement agents?" I asked her. Julius, her fiancé who was also a witch, worked for them, running down cases as a magical detective of sorts, but he didn't wear a robe or drive an ominous car and pull over innocent witches. "I know they have teams that go out and pick up suspects, like when they apprehended Harper today, but flashing lights and sticky magic? I've never heard of that before."

Suspects? Were we suspects for something? For the past few months, I hadn't done much of anything other than work a few shifts at the Grind. I'd outfitted the nursery in the spare room at home and started experimenting with mild herb blends designed to help promote mental and physical well-being to maybe sell at Bea's shop. But other than that, I'd been downright boring. Why would I be a suspect in anything?

I glanced at my friend. "Pyper?"

"Yeah?" Her fingers had tightened around the wheel, and a sheen of sweat had popped out on her forehead. I couldn't tell if that was from nerves or the overwhelming, hellish temperatures in August in New Orleans.

"You haven't been up to anything... unusual lately have you?"

She turned and met my gaze. "You mean other than wedding planning and making a hundred protection charms for the reception?"

My lips twitched. Instead of giving something to promote love and happiness, Pyper and Julius were handing out pendants that were designed to protect people from evil spirits. Being that Pyper was a medium and Julius had spent a significant amount of time as a ghost in his previous life, they were both a little more paranoid about evil spirits than the average supernatural. "Yes, other than that."

"Nope. The last trouble that found me was that curse, and it affected Bo, not me. The only thing I think I can be accused of is drinking too much coffee and indulging Ida May's inappropriate sexual innuendo." Ida May was the resident ghost at the Grind. She was known for arranging pastries in a sexually suggestive way while also writing not-safe-for-work messages on the specials board.

A man in a purple robe with long, bony fingers tapped on my window, making me jump. "Hell on fire," I breathed and pressed the button to lower the window, trying to keep my magic from shorting out the electrical system of Kane's car.

"Mrs. Rouquette?" the man asked, crouching down to peer into the window. His face was so white he seemed almost ghostly, and he had a thin smile and beady, dark brown eyes.

"It's Ms. Calhoun, but I am married to Kane Rouquette," I said, fear suddenly making my stomach churn. Did this have to do with the Brotherhood? Had Kane been called to deal with another demon while Pyper and I had been visiting Mati? "Is this about Kane? Is he okay? What happened?"

"Kane?" the man asked, confusion rolling off him in waves as he glanced at the electronic device in his hand. His eyes narrowed, and when he glanced back at me, all the kindness was gone and replaced with pure disdain. "Demon hunter. No wonder. Okay." He opened my door and ordered, "Out of the car."

I clutched Flame closer and glared at the man. "Not until you tell us who you are and why you forced us to pull over."

"I'm an agent of the Witches' Council, and you Mrs. Rouq—err, Ms. Calhoun, have been summoned for questioning. You can either get out of the car and come with us peacefully or I can magically bind you and force you. Your choice."

So they *were* from the council. Was this division new? I'd never heard of them before, but that didn't exactly mean very much. The council was a secretive bunch who were charged with overseeing the magical community and policing black-magic users. They were also the keepers of magical relics and weapons. But I wasn't a black-magic user. I was a white witch and one of the good guys. "You do realize I'm the New Orleans coven leader, right?" I asked, my tone full of righteous indignation.

He gave me a flat stare. "And I'm the king of the Krewe of Ghoul. So what? You're still wanted for questioning. Are you cooperating or are you going to make this difficult?"

Everything inside me screamed to resist, and if I hadn't been seven months pregnant, I just might have. But as I was getting ready to open my mouth and tell him to shove his questions where the sun didn't shine, my little girl kicked at my ribs and thick, dark gray rain clouds rolled overhead. I glanced up, knowing that the peanut and I had caused the weather change. It happened lately, especially when I was upset.

"Jade," Pyper said gently. "Why don't we just go to the council and let them ask their questions? It's not like you did anything or even know anything, right?"

I turned and looked into her brilliant blue eyes. "We don't even know what this is about."

She cut her gaze to Flame and then back to me and raised one eyebrow.

I shrugged, unable to answer her unasked question. If I had to guess, I'd say this had everything to do with Harper, but there was no way to find out unless I went with them. And the fact was we both knew that if I resisted, they'd force me anyway. Crap. I really had no choice.

I turned my attention back to the witch glaring at me. "Can we at least follow you there? I'm not under arrest or anything, am I?"

He took another look at his electronic device. "Says here you must be taken into custody. You'll be released after our questions are answered."

I ground my teeth. "I'm not talking without a lawyer present."

"This isn't a court of law, Ms. Calhoun. The mundane laws don't apply at the council."

I knew that, of course. I'd already stood "trial" with them once before. Lucien had been my representative. Still, I wasn't navigating this alone. "Pyper, call Lucien. Tell him to meet me there." Then I handed her Flame. "Take care of this one and call Kane. Tell him what's happening."

"I'm on it," she said, already tapping on her phone.

I swung my legs out of the car and barked at the council witch. "You better take a step back unless you want me to tackle you. A seven-months-pregnant witch needs a little space to haul herself out of a car."

He glanced down at my belly and frowned. "Son of Zeus.

You'd think you witches could take a break from bullshit for at least a few months while you're pregnant. At least until the baby's born. Don't you care at all about what happens to it?"

Rage surged through my veins. His disgust was crawling all over me, and my skin itched with it. I grabbed the frame of the door and hauled myself out of the car, spitting mad. "My baby isn't an *it*. *She* is a baby girl, and there isn't anything in this world I wouldn't do to protect her. And that includes cursing the man bits of a self-righteous asshole who has no ever-loving clue what he's talking about. Now step off before I shrivel your member into a brittle piece of charred leather just because you opened your mouth and spoke without letting your brain in on the decision."

"Oh, Jade. Christ," Pyper said from inside the car with a chuckle. But then she let out a sigh and added, "That's probably not going to help matters."

"No it isn't," the council witch said, grabbing my wrist and twisting me around so that my hand was behind my back.

My instincts kicked in, and the magic I'd been holding in check burst from my free hand. Only instead of shooting straight toward the witch's chest as I'd intended, my magic fizzled and faded into the ether, impotent and useless. Then I felt it. A neutralizing band had already been slapped around my wrist, causing that small flame of magic that flickered inside me to vanish. The baby kicked harder, and I doubled over, holding my stomach with my free hand.

The sun beat down on my neck, and I knew the rain

clouds had vanished. The baby kicked again, letting me know she was not at all happy with this new development. I couldn't blame her. I wasn't fond of it myself.

"That's quite enough," I said through clenched teeth. "I said I'd go with you. There's no reason to manhandle me."

"Right." The witch grabbed my other hand, secured it with magical zip ties, and hauled me to the black sedan, making me stumble slightly over the pavement.

A group of people had gathered on the nearby porch of a shotgun double house. A woman wearing too-short shorts and a bikini top took a drag of her cigarette, her eyes focused on the witch opening the back door of the car.

After blowing out the smoke, she took a step forward and leaned over her railing. "What's wrong with you, mister? You can't restrain a pregnant lady with her hands tied behind her back. If she falls forward and hurts herself or the baby, your department is gonna be in deep shit."

"Mind your own business," the council witch said and shoved me forward again.

My toe hit something hard, and I started to fall forward. I thrashed as I instinctively tried to pull my hands free of my restraints to break my fall. But fear rendered me nearly paralyzed as I realized there was no way that was going to happen. The asphalt was coming far too fast, and my belly was going to break my fall.

Only just before I hit belly-first on the hot ground, strong hands grabbed my shoulders, holding me up. Instead, my knees hit the road and pain radiated through my kneecaps, but my only cry was one of relief. My peanut was safe. At least for now. I glanced over my shoulder at a second witch, a younger, larger one with dark skin, who was gently lifting me back to my feet.

"I told you so," the woman with the cigarette said in disgust. "You hurt her and her child and that is gonna be one helluva lawsuit."

The jerk who'd manhandled me shouted, "Mind your own business or you'll be dragged in, too."

A string of colorful curses left her lips, but sudden waves of fear rippled from the porch, and the group slipped back into the house. New Orleans law enforcement wasn't exactly known for their stellar ethics. No one wanted to mess with them especially if they had a less than squeaky-clean record. I couldn't blame any of them for backing off.

"Are you all right, Ms. Calhoun?" the man steadying me asked, his voice soft and full of concern.

"She's fine. Just put her in the car," my abuser ordered.

"Cool it, Fitch," the second one barked. His hands touched my wrists and the restraints vanished, freeing my hands. But before I could call my magic, ice-cold bands snaked around each one, cutting off my ability to use the power still flowing in my veins. "We can't have you cursing us," he said pleasantly in my ear. "But I see no need to treat you with anything less than respect."

I supposed I should've been grateful. He'd certainly been the voice of reason between the two, but just because he was playing good cop didn't mean I trusted him. "There's no need for any of this," I spat out. "If the council has questions, I would've come in willingly. I don't have anything to hide."

"That's what they all say, Ms. Calhoun," Good Cop said. "But I'm sure you realize that in our position, we just can't take chances. You coven witches are far too resourceful. Now, please do me a favor and don't fight me on this. I'd rather we just all calmly go to the council without any other hassles."

Since I'd already been manhandled and almost toppled over belly-first, I gritted my teeth and calmly climbed into the back of the car. "Pyper?"

"Yes," she was standing off to the side, her expression set in a scowl. I imagined if my magical gifts were working that a red tornado of anger would be swirling around her. "I'm right here."

"Will you follow us to the council?" I asked her.

"Of course." She glared at the two witches still hovering over my open door.

"There's no need—" Good Cop started, but I cut him off.

"Yes. There is. I don't want anyone to get 'lost' on the way to the council headquarters." I glanced over at Pyper once more. "Call Bea on the way. I want her to know where I am and how I got there."

Pyper, who already had her phone in her hand, tapped the screen. Just as she spoke into the phone, Flame shot out of the car and went for Fitch's leg. Her teeth sank in, and Fitch kicked out and roared.

The dog went flying, landing right at Pyper's feet. Flame spun around and let out a stream of fire, scorching the patch of grass lining the sidewalk.

"Get that demon," Fitch ordered Good Cop. "Now. It needs to be eliminated before it hurts someone."

"It's not a demon," I cried, certain he was wrong. I'd felt demon energy before. It didn't resemble the dog's at all.

"Yes, it is," Fitch snarled. "Only demons can breathe fire."

And dragons, I thought to myself. But it wasn't a dragon either. A dragon's familiar? A magical creature that had been spelled to breathe fire? I had no idea other than it for sure wasn't a demon, and they weren't going to destroy it if I had anything to say about it. Not that I was in any position to help at the moment.

But Pyper was. Without missing a beat, she bent down, picked up the dog, and whirled around. In a flash, she was back in Kane's car with the door shut. She turned the engine over with Flame still sitting in her lap and growling at Fitch through the window.

Fitch reached for the door handle, jerking on the latch, but it was obviously locked. Pyper put up her middle finger and glared. That probably wasn't the most productive move ever, but it still gave me a petty sense of satisfaction. These agents were completely over the line, hauling me off to the council when I hadn't done anything other than take care of a fire-breathing dog.

Gray magic seeped from Fitch's fingertips, and in the next moment, the door swung open and he hauled Pyper out. His ugly, pasty-white hand was gripping her arm as he reached into the car for Flame. The dog opened her maw and let out a flash of fire, singeing his robes.

He jumped back, using Pyper as a shield. But the second she was in the dog's line of fire, Flame closed her mouth and darted out of the car, disappearing behind it.

"That thing had better run. The minute I get my hands on it, it's dead," Fitch said through clenched teeth, dragging

Pyper to the car I was sitting in. She stumbled and was unable to get her feet back under her.

"Stop!" she ordered, her feet scrambling to find purchase.

The magic inside me strained for release. I was spitting mad, so angry that I could barely think straight. My senses were too clouded.

"Let go of her," I ordered, but neither of the witches were listening to me. Fitch was hauling Pyper to the other side of the car, her hands restrained behind her back, while Good Cop shook his head and sighed.

"Was that necessary?" Good Cop asked Fitch.

"Yes," he said, not bothering to explain himself. He opened the car door and shoved her in beside me.

"Oomph," she said and winced as her head grazed the doorframe on her way down.

"Dammit. What is wrong with you, *Fitch?*" I asked. "Pyper is just a bystander. Why is she being hauled in?"

Fitch ignored her and slipped into the driver's seat.

Good Cop took his place beside him and glanced over his shoulder. "Are you all right, Ms. Rayne?"

"No, I'm not all right. I probably have a lump on my head, and I'm being hauled into the Witches' Council. I'm not even a witch. This is bullshit, and I demand a lawyer."

It didn't escape my notice that they already knew who she was. That probably meant they knew she was Julius's fiancée. But why would they mess with the future spouse of a fellow witch who worked at the council?

"Here." Fitch tossed Pyper's phone to Good Cop. "Hold

on to this. Find out who she called so we know who to expect."

Good Cop glanced at it and scowled. "Beatrice Kelton. Fuck me. She's going to be trouble."

I sent the witch a self-satisfied smile. Damn straight she was. Bea didn't fuck around. "I hope you're ready for her."

They both ignored me as Fitch put the car in gear and hauled us off to the council. I eyed Kane's car as we sped past the Lexus. The door was still open, and likely still running from when Pyper cranked the engine. I cringed. There was a really good chance the car would be jacked within minutes. But there was one small victory. Flame had found her way back into the car, and neither Fitch nor Good Cop had noticed. Good. At least she was safe... for now.

CHAPTER 5

"It's a good thing you stuffed yourself full of carbs earlier," Pyper said, pressing her hand to her stomach as it growled with hunger. "How long do you think we've been stuck in here?"

"A few hours maybe?" I shifted on the wooden bench, trying to ease the ache in my backside. We were in a barren holding cell with just the bench along one wall and a sink in the corner. No other bathroom facilities. Which was starting to become an issue. I hauled myself up to my feet and started to pace, hoping to take my mind off my bladder.

"I'm going to pass out if I don't get a sandwich soon," Pyper said, pressing her fingertips to her temples.

I moved to the cell door and eyed the guard at the end of the hall. "I need a restroom."

He stared straight ahead and ignored me.

"And I need a burger," Pyper called.

I glanced over at her. "When's the last time you ate?"

"I had a yogurt for breakfast."

"I'd have died by now."

"You'd have eaten your own hand by now." She got up and moved to stand next to me. "Yo, asshat," she called to the guard. "We have needs. Food and bathroom breaks are imperative."

No answer. He didn't even twitch. It was as if he couldn't hear us at all.

"Get someone down here within the next five minutes, or I'm going to tell everyone about your plushie fetish," Pyper said.

"What?" His head snapped up for the first time since we'd been unceremoniously dumped into the cell.

"You know, the brightly colored ponies tucked into the bottom drawer of your nightstand?" She narrowed her eyes and added in a fake seductive tone, "And the fact that the fuchsia one is your favorite."

"I... What? You... That's ridiculous," he sputtered, glancing around him as if someone had just spilled all his deepest darkest secrets.

If I had to guess, I'd say that someone *was* spilling all his secrets to Pyper. Only that someone was a ghost only Pyper could hear. And whoever they were, they were giving Pyper all the ammunition she needed to get under the guy's skin. Which would mean he really did have a plushie fetish. Ew.

I grimaced and shook my head at him. "Plushies? Really?"

His face turned bright red and he stammered again. "I-I'm, uh, be right back."

Pyper and I were silent as he struggled with the key in

the door. Once he finally got it open, he tripped over his own feet as he scrambled out.

The door slammed shut and Pyper said, "Thanks, Kimmy." After a moment, Pyper laughed. "Oh, good one. I'll keep that tidbit in my back pocket in case I need it later."

"New friend?" I asked her.

She smirked. "Kimmy used to own the creepy guard's old Victorian in Mid-City. She doesn't like him much. Says he does a shoddy job of maintaining her house. Apparently he doesn't fix anything. The leak in the roof ruined the wallpaper she put up herself in the master bathroom twenty-five years ago, and she is *not* happy about it. She's been dunking his toothbrush in the toilet for months now."

"Oh, gross." I pressed one hand to my belly and tried not to gag at the thought.

"Yeah. Really gross. But he hasn't noticed, so it's been a quiet rebellion. She was more than happy to tell me about his... ah, private desires." She cackled. "Kimmy is ready to haunt his ugly ass for the next hundred years if he doesn't find some way to let us out of here. She's particularly worried about you, mama-to-be."

"Thanks, Kimmy," I said, raising my voice. "The peanut and I appreciate the help."

Pyper cocked an ear, chuckled, and nodded. "Kimmy says he's begging someone to move us to a conference room as we speak. Apparently he's terrified we'll say something about his pony collection."

I squeezed my eyes shut, trying to force the vision of molested stuffed ponies out of my mind. It was the most disturbing thing I'd heard in months.

The door swung open, and steps clattered on the stone floor.

Madam Tempest rounded the corner wearing a red velvet robe and black lace-up boots. Her white hair was piled on her head in an elaborate braid. If it hadn't been for her red face and angry expression, I'd have thought she looked magnificent. Instead, she just looked downright sinister with her tight lips and icy glare.

"Ms. Calhoun. You had better have answers, otherwise you're in for an extended stay." She glanced at my swollen belly and scowled. "Dammit. Blaine, take them to the interrogation room on the fifth floor. Make sure there's water and something to eat." And without waiting for me to say a word, she spun on her heel and disappeared into thin air.

Pyper turned to me, her eyebrows raised. "That was an interesting trick."

I just shrugged. All I cared about was a bathroom and whatever they had for snacks. The peanut was hungry again.

"I'm not answering any questions until I get a bathroom break," I demanded, refusing to sit down in the interrogation room.

"Ms. Calhoun, I don't have the authority to—"

"Do you want me to go right here?" I glared at the young witch who was wringing her hands. She couldn't have been more than twenty and was obviously completely out of her element. If I didn't get a restroom soon, we were going to have a situation on our hands. "Have you ever been pregnant?"

"No, ma'am." She bit her bottom lip and eyed my belly.

Ma'am? Was she serious? I was only about ten years older than her. But that was the south for you. "Then you have no idea what it's like to have a melon sitting on your bladder, do you? Get me to a restroom now, or you're gonna have to clean up my mess."

"I'd do what she says if I were you," Pyper said with a nod "Last week we got caught in traffic, and let's just say that car is still at the professional car wash getting detailed." She smiled sweetly at the witch.

I bit my cheek to keep from laughing. Her story was a complete lie, but it was worth it to see the witch pale as she looked at me. I shrugged.

"Come with me," she said, grabbing my arm.

My wrists had been bound with magical bands, keeping me from using my magic, but at least they were free and I wasn't shackled like a hardened criminal.

"Just don't try anything," the young witch pleaded. "If anything happens, they'll blame me and lock me up next."

"Why? What's going on?" None of this made sense. Pyper and I hadn't done anything to warrant this treatment, except for maybe having a strange fire-breathing dog hanging around. But even that didn't warrant this level of crazy from the council.

"I can't..." She glanced around, her eyes wide, and lowered her voice. "It's better if I don't talk about it."

I placed a light hand on her arm. Even though my

empath abilities had been dampened due to the bands on my wrists, it wasn't hard to figure out that this witch was on the verge of panic. "It's all right. You can tell me. I'm not the enemy. What's your name?"

"Kinsley." She glanced over her shoulder and then nodded to the unmarked door in front of us. "That's the restroom."

Relief rushed through me, and my eyes started to water with pure relief as I hurried in. "Oh, thank the goddess."

When I finally emerged, feeling like a new woman, I found Kinsley leaning against the counter, her arms crossed over her chest and staring at the floor. As I washed my hands, I glanced over at her. "You can tell me whatever it is that's bothering you, you know. I'm a good listener."

She let out a huff of humorless laughter. "If I tell you, I'll lose my job, but if I don't, I won't be able to look at myself in the mirror anymore."

I froze, water dripping from my clean hands. "It sounds like there's something important I should know."

She raised her head and stared me straight in the eye. "It's about your friend, Harper."

I blinked. I'd just met Harper. I'd hardly call her a friend. But I wasn't going to tell Kinsley that. Whatever she had to say, I wanted to hear it. "What about her?"

"She disappeared, and the council thinks you had a hand in it."

"Disappeared?" I asked with a small gasp. "What do you mean? I saw them haul her away."

She nodded. "Right. They locked her in a holding cell

while they were processing her. And when they came back to get her for questioning, she was gone."

I frowned, trying to understand what I had to do with any of this. "How long ago was that?"

After clearing her throat, she cupped her mouth with one hand and whispered, "It happened right before they dispatched Fitch and Myers to pick you up. They think you had something to do with it."

"Me?" I practically yelled as I straightened my shoulders. "How could I—?"

"Shhh!" She pressed her hand over my mouth. "If they find out I told you anything, I'll be in that cell beside you." After a moment, she removed her hand and took a step back.

"Right." I narrowed my eyes and studied her. "Why did you tell me?"

She shrugged. "You just seem… I don't know. It doesn't feel like something you did."

The way she said the words made me think that her feeling might be more than just normal intuition. Like maybe she had some sort of supernatural power that let her read people's energy or intentions or something. "Well, you're right. I don't know anything about that. I don't even know why she was arrested."

Kinsley studied me intently and then shook her head. "That's not the entire truth, is it?"

I bit back the chuckle threatening to break through. She was a truth seeker. Interesting. "It's mostly the truth. All I know is what was said when she was taken. Something about 'seeking to unleash the dragon,' whatever that means."

"Okay," she said with a nod. "I buy that."

"Kinsley," I said, wishing I could read her energy. "Are you a witch?"

"Nah." She stared down at her feet, her face flushing pink. "I just... I can sense things."

I'd been that girl. The one who could only sense things about people. But when I met Bea, she helped me uncover my hidden talents, and it turned out I was a powerful white witch. And even though my magic was cut off at the moment, something told me the girl in front of me was oozing with some sort of power. There was a lot more to her than just sensing truth. "Have you ever tried to explore your abilities? See if there's more to tap into?"

A pained expression flashed over her face and she started to shake her head, but suddenly she froze, and her eyes widened. "We have to go." Grabbing my arm, she started to pull me out of the restroom. "Madam Tempest is on her way."

"So?" I asked as I let her guide me back to the interrogation room. "She didn't seem to be in a hurry before."

"She was dealing with something important. Come on. I'll be in trouble if you aren't there."

I should have been annoyed. After hours of waiting and being denied a restroom, I shouldn't have wanted to help any of them, but Kinsley had shown compassion when it was clear she was disobeying orders. So I quickened my pace, and as soon as we slipped back into the interrogation room, I touched her arm. "My offer stands. If you want to explore your power, find me when this is over."

"Why?" she asked, her tone incredulous. "After the way you've been treated… I'd think you wouldn't want anything to do with anyone here."

I gave her a gentle smile. "I have friends who work for the council. Nothing is black and white. I know there are good people here."

She returned my smile with a genuine one of her own, nodded to Pyper, and then disappeared.

Pyper raised one eyebrow, silently questioning the exchange.

"She's just a kid doing her job," I said, eyeing a cup of water and a sad-looking packet of crackers on the table. There was a discarded plastic wrapper and empty cup in front of Pyper. Clearly someone had brought us some rations. It wasn't nearly enough to wipe out my hunger, but I grabbed the crackers anyway, ate them like I was a starving woman, and gulped the water entirely too fast before I said, "Kinsley's a kid with a unique ability. I'd love to explore what else she can do."

"Why?" Pyper leaned back in her chair.

"I don't know… I guess—" Shaking my head, I let out a small laugh. "I think she reminds me of me before I embraced my witchy side. Only not quite as clueless. I just think her ability is interesting."

"You want a project," Pyper said. "You haven't been working the past few months, and now you're bored. Life isn't exciting enough."

I glanced around the white room. "All signs say otherwise at the moment."

"Yeah, yeah. We both know we'll be out of here this

afternoon. One way or another. Since we didn't do anything, they have no reason to keep us here."

"Or so you think, Ms. Rayne," Madam Tempest said from behind me.

I turned and eyed the white-haired woman. She'd just appeared in the doorway, her lips set into a grim line.

"Madam Tempest," I said, not bothering to hide my irritation. "Want to tell us why we're here? It's not exactly standard practice to arrest the white witch of New Orleans without grounds, is it?"

"White witch," she said, her tone taking on an air of derision. "Your status has no bearing here, Ms. Calhoun." She waved a hand. "Have a seat. We have things to discuss."

"No bearing," Pyper mimicked. "Isn't that fun?"

I shot her a look that said *not now* and took a seat at the table. At least the plastic chairs were more comfortable than the wooden bench we'd been sitting on earlier. "Well, I'm on pins and needles. What is it you think we did?"

She sat across from us, placed her forearms on the table, and clasped her hands together, staring me down. "I need to know where Harper Spelling is. It's a crucial matter to the city, Ms. Calhoun."

Half a dozen responses were on the tip of my tongue, but I bit them back. The council wasn't to be trusted. They'd already proven to be one of the paranormal entities who played by their own rules. "I'm not saying anything until I have representation."

"We aren't the NOPD, Ms. Calhoun," she said impatiently. "Lawyers won't help you here."

"No, but witches who understand the legalities of the

paranormal world will. I want Lucien Boulard or Beatrice Kelton before I say another word."

"What she said," Pyper added, pointing at me.

Madam Tempest glared at both of us. "I'd rather you didn't play games with me."

"Games?" My eyebrows shot up, and my irritation flared. "You think I'm playing some sort of game with you? I'm seven months pregnant, Madam Tempest. I have been actively trying to stay out of magical matters ever since the dragon soul debacle. In fact, all I've been doing the past few months is planning my best friend's wedding, her bridal shower, and her bachelorette party. Today we were buying novelty dildos at an adult shop, and that was the first time we met Harper. How could I possibly have any idea where she is?"

The council witch's lips twitched into the barest whisper of a satisfied smile.

Dammit. I wasn't supposed to say anything, was I?

"Only you can say for sure why you might know where she is." Tempest reached into a pocket of her red velvet robe and extracted a small notebook. "Your name, address, phone number, and a sketch of you is in this book we confiscated from Ms. Spelling. You are listed with a handful of other people who are labeled as dragon leaders. Everyone else's names have been crossed out. Yours is circled."

"Dragon leader?" I glanced at Pyper, noting the confusion I felt was mirrored in her expression. "You know the only interaction I've ever had with dragons was when dealing with Conor. I'm a witch, not some dragon leader, whatever that means."

She glanced over her shoulder and said, "Kinsley? What do you think?"

My head snapped up, and I spotted the young witch who'd escorted me to the restroom. She'd somehow slipped back into the room without my noticing. I glanced at the bands on my wrists and scowled. That never would've happened if my magic weren't neutralized. Not that I'd said anything that she couldn't hear. I just hated that I hadn't sensed her.

"She's telling the truth," Kinsley said so quietly I barely made out her words.

"And her friend? Does she know anything?" Tempest asked.

Kinsley shrugged. "Doubtful, but you haven't directly asked her."

"Ms. Rayne," Tempest said. "Have you had any dealings with Harper Spelling at any time other than this morning at her place of business?"

"Not that I'm aware of," Pyper said, leaning back in her chair and crossing her arms over her chest. "You do realize that I don't have magic, right? There's no way I've had anything to do with dragons."

Tempest nodded. "I am. You're a medium though, correct?"

"Yes." Pyper sent me a questioning glance.

I shrugged, having no idea why the witch was asking about her abilities.

"Good. You'll both be working for the council until this case is solved." She held out her hand to Kinsley, who passed her a folder.

"Wait, what?" I asked, sitting forward. "I'm giving birth in a couple of months. I've already taken leave from my job."

"Then you won't have any conflicts to keep you from tracking Harper down." She placed a sheet of paper in front of me and one in front of Pyper.

Pyper grabbed it and scanned the sheet. Just as I picked mine up, Pyper let out a curse and said, "Are you kidding me? If we don't bring her in, we'll be charged with obstruction and assault of a council witch?"

"What?" I quickly found the terms of the contract. Basically she wanted us to find Harper, turn her over to the council, and then we were free. If not, they'd lock us up and make us wait for a council trial. I'd spend the last two months of my pregnancy in the council jail. "Obstruction of what?" I demanded.

"Obstruction of our investigation of course," she said as if it were obvious. "You did take the dragon familiar in without notifying us, didn't you?"

"I knew that dog was a familiar," I said under my breath.

She nodded. "You should have brought her in right away. She could be the key to finding Harper, and now she's just running around the city, a danger to everyone if she decides to unleash her fire." Tempest tapped the paper in front of me. "Sign the contract and you and your friend are free to go. If not, I'll have Kinsley get your cells ready."

"Shit." Pyper ran a hand through her dark hair. The blue streak in front fell over her left eye as she scowled. "You realize I have a business to manage, right?" she asked Tempest. "I can't just run around the city, looking for some girl you couldn't even keep locked in a cell."

61

"Your business will have to find a way to run without you. Either way, you'll be unavailable for the foreseeable future." Madam Tempest got up. "I'll give you a few minutes to weigh your options."

She swept out of the room with Kinsley right behind her.

"They can't do this," Pyper said, jumping to her feet and pacing around the room. "We're basically admitting guilt if we sign these forms."

"You're right, but I don't see that we have any other choice, do you?" We were innocent but even if we did get a lawyer to fight this, the council would drag out the proceedings for months, leaving us locked up for who knew how long. The council didn't operate the same way as the mundane legal system. They tended to do whatever they pleased, and I couldn't let that happen, not while pregnant. My head started to spin. The cracker and cup of water hadn't done anything to help my blood sugar. If we didn't get out of there soon, I was going to pass out.

"I'm going to demand to see Lucien or Bea or even Julius before we sign these forms." She let out a low growl. "I understand her obsession with you, but why does she want me?"

"It's for your medium gift," that quiet voice said again.

I jumped and nearly slid right out of the chair. "Holy hell, Kinsley. You almost gave me a heart attack."

"Because I can talk to ghosts? What does that have to do with anything?" Pyper asked, her eyes glued to Kinsley.

"I have the files on Harper," Kinsley said as she took a seat. "But I can't let you see them unless you sign the contracts. Trust me. Your gift is going to come in really handy."

"You mean the reason we're here at all is because Tempest wants Pyper and not me?" I asked hopefully. It would be nice for a change to not be the one that was always attracting all the trouble.

Kinsley let out a humorless laugh. "No. You're the witch who contained a dragon a few months ago. You're just about the only one anyone here thinks can contain this situation. Believe me when I say she won't let this go until you sign on."

"What could she possibly do besides slap us with these bogus charges?" Pyper asked, still pacing.

"She can delay the hearing." Kinsley glanced at me. "And I think she will, despite Jade's condition. There's too much at stake. She'll do anything it takes to get what she wants."

"And that is?" I asked.

"Harper. The council needs to bring her in. As soon as possible."

Pyper finally stopped pacing and asked, "What did she do?"

Kinsley glanced from Pyper to me and then back at Pyper. "She set a curse in motion to unleash the dragons."

"What does that mean exactly," I asked. "What dragons?"

Her lips formed a thin line, and she seemed to contemplate whether she was going to tell us or not. But then, finally, she took a deep breath and said, "The ones that were awakened two months ago when the dragon got loose and called them home."

CHAPTER 6

*I*n the end, we didn't talk to anyone. Not Lucien. Not Bea. And not Julius. However, after we signed the paperwork and were released, all three of them plus Kane were pacing the front lobby, waiting for us.

"Jade. My god. Are you all right?" Kane asked, putting his arm around my shoulders and pulling me in close to him.

"Yeah, but I'm starving, and I could probably drink a gallon of water," I said, leaning into him and trying to ignore the pent-up frustration that was simmering beneath his surface. The magical bands that had been containing my magic were gone, and everyone's emotions were running high, threatening to overwhelm me.

"Here, Jade," Bea said, handing me a bag of her homemade trail mix. "This should help."

I took the bag of nuts and dried fruit and gobbled down a handful. When I glanced back up, she handed me a bottle of water. "Thank you."

"Come on. Let's go get some actual food," Pyper said, dragging Julius out of the lobby of the council offices.

The rest of us followed, and I was surprised to find that Kane already had the Lexus back. "How'd you know where to find it?" I asked him.

"Mati and Vaughn. They called not long after you were taken in." He opened the door for me, and I glanced around, looking for Flame. "Where's the dog? Didn't they pick her up too?"

He raised both eyebrows. "The fire-breathing one?"

"Yeah. That one. She tried to turn the council witches into crispy-fried assholes and then took off before they could apprehend her. But I saw her curled up in the car as we drove away."

"Mati didn't say anything about her. I'm not sure they even know she's on the loose."

"Great," I whispered as I let my head flop back against the headrest. "One more thing to worry about."

BEA BUSTLED around her bright kitchen while Lucien set a plate of cheese and crackers on the table. Discussing the supernatural and actual dragons in a public place wasn't an option, so Bea had led us to her place and had graciously offered to feed us. She'd already set out a pitcher of homemade lemonade, and Pyper and I were busy chowing down on the cheese and crackers while Lucien, Julius, and Kane vented about the council.

"I've never known them to coerce someone to work for

them before," Lucien said, his face taking on a red tinge from his anger. "It's unethical."

Julius let out a bark of humorless laughter. "I have. The problem with the council elders is that they don't have anyone to answer to. When they get a bee buzzing in their ass, they've been known to pull all kinds of shit until they get what they want."

Bea set a bowl of potato salad on the table. "Julius is right. It's why I broke ties with them years ago."

"The charges are relatively minor and wouldn't amount to much even if they did decide to rule against you both. But they definitely could've pulled all kinds of shit to delay the hearing. I think you probably made the best choice, choosing to track Harper down. You were already working on finding out what was going on anyway, right?" Lucien asked as he pulled out a leather-bound notebook.

"Jade definitely was in investigation mode," Pyper said.

I scooped a large spoonful of potato salad and dropped it onto my plate. "There was talk about dragons. All I wanted to do was make sure we didn't end up with another one terrorizing New Orleans."

Kane put his hand on my knee and refilled my lemonade glass. "No surprise there. My girl would never be able to ignore something like that."

I smiled up at him, my heart swelling with love. He knew and accepted me even while it was clear to me he really would prefer I stay locked in the house until our daughter was born. The great thing about Kane was that he respected me and my judgment. I wasn't about to hide out while anyone was in danger. We'd tried that once. It hadn't worked out. Besides, I was stronger than ever at the moment. Other than the council threatening my freedom, I wasn't in any danger. Not yet anyway. When it came to magic, nothing was certain. But I would do my best to keep myself out of trouble.

While I dug into the potato salad, Pyper flipped the folder open that Kinsley had given us.

"What's it say?" I asked between bites.

"Not much. Just a background check on Harper and a copy of the contents of her notebook." Pyper shuffled through the papers and handed half to Julius, who was to her left. "Doesn't look like a lot to go on."

Bea placed a tray of croissant sandwiches on the table and sat next to me. "I'm sorry you got dragged into this."

I gave her a small smile. "Occupational hazard I suppose."

She chuckled. "Coven leaders do usually see more than their share of trouble."

"You survived," I said and grabbed a roast beef sandwich.

"And so will you." She winked and filled her glass with lemonade.

"Whoa," Julius said. "Pyper, did you see this?" He leaned over, showing her one of the pieces of paper.

"No." She scanned it, and her eyes widened. "Harper's a known medium as well?"

"Says she worked for the coven leader of Salem for a while before she moved to New Orleans," Julius said.

"That's interesting," I said. "She told us she has an aunt who's a witch and owns a novelty shop in Salem."

Julius shook his head. "That's not entirely true. Her aunt

is the coven leader. She owns a haunted inn and has been making money on the side selling love potions, psychic readings, and herb curses."

"That sounds kinda shady," I said. "Curses? From a coven leader?" I glanced at Bea. "That's pretty unethical, isn't it?"

She nodded. "If they're minor curses, it might sound worse than it is. If they're fake, then she's just a scammer. If she's dabbling in black magic..." Bea pressed her lips into a thin line. "Then that's something the council would've looked into. Or should unless there's some corruption going on up there."

"So it's either shady or downright evil. Not a good sign." I picked at the croissant, troubled that Harper had lied to me. I'd liked her when we'd met and had been giving her the benefit of the doubt. But maybe I was wrong. If she'd worked for her shady aunt, maybe she *was* trying to unleash dragons.

"I don't understand how she was able to escape the council," Pyper said, her brows pinched as she handed me the files. "If she's just a medium, she wouldn't have been able to magic herself out of there."

A bark of laughter escaped from the back of my throat. "Hell, I'm a coven leader, and even I can't magic myself out of there."

"She must've had help," Bea said.

"Maybe a ghost let her out," Pyper said.

Everyone was silent for a moment while we stared at Pyper.

"What?" she asked.

"Did you see or hear any ghosts while we were there, other than Kimmy?" I asked.

She shook her head. "No, but I wasn't listening for any. But you did last time you were there," she pointed out.

"True." I chewed on that information. "Kinsley said that Pyper's skill would come in handy. Maybe that's what she meant. Maybe we need to go back to the council offices and hunt some ghosts."

Pyper groaned. "Today?"

"No." Kane put his arm across the back of my chair. "It's late and I'm taking Jade home. Tomorrow you can start the Harper hunt."

"Tomorrow. Definitely." I stifled a yawn. "We can go back to the Witches' Council and check out the new recruits for Mati's sorority. See if anyone knows anything."

"I'll do some research of my own," Lucien said, pushing his chair back and standing.

"Thanks," I said, grateful my second-in-command always had my back.

He cleared his throat and added, "I think Kat is expecting you both for lunch tomorrow."

Son of a... He was right. We were supposed to finalize the details for her wedding shower that I was hosting at my house on Saturday. I'd debated just taking care of all the details myself, but Kat had very specific ideas about what she wanted for her wedding festivities, and rather than get it wrong, I'd decided to just loop her in on everything. So far that had proved to be the right decision.

"Of course," I said. "We'll be there, right Pyper?"

She pulled her phone out and tapped the screen. "Got it

right here. Lunch. One o'clock at the sushi place in the CBD."

Lucien let out a breath and his shoulders relaxed as he gave us a hint of a smile. "Good. That's good. I know she's looking forward to it."

I touched his arm. "Tell her we missed her today. And that I'm fine. So she doesn't need to run over and check on me."

He chuckled. "I'll tell her, but no promises."

Kane stood up and walked him to the door. "Tell her if she's coming to come soon. I'm putting Jade to bed early tonight."

Pyper leaned across the table and whispered, "After he gets you into that lacy black number."

I rolled my eyes. "That's probably the last thing on his mind."

She glanced over at Kane and then back to me. "No, it isn't." Laughing, she stood and held her hand out to Julius. "Take me home, babe. I'm ready to throw pizza money at Bo and make it an early night."

"I'll meet you at the Grind at nine," I said as they headed for the door.

Pyper threw one hand up, indicating she'd heard me, and a moment later it was just me, Kane, and Bea.

I glanced at my mentor. "What do you think? Is it possible dragons were awakened?"

She picked up the tray of leftover sandwiches. "Anything is possible when it comes to magic and the supernatural. You know that, Jade."

"That's what I was afraid of." I pushed my chair back and

started to help her clear the table.

"I've got this," Bea said, gently taking the plate from me. She placed a soft hand on my arm and smiled down at my belly. "Go on home and take care of that baby growing in there."

"No, we should—"

"Go home and get some rest," she insisted. "Besides, Maximus will be here soon. He's excellent at clearing tables."

I giggled at the image of the Brotherhood leader clearing her table. "I guess it's good for him to be domestic every now and then."

"He sure isn't at the Brotherhood headquarters," Kane said, slipping his arm around me. "A little domesticity is good for a powerful leader." He winked at me. "Right, love?"

"I have no idea," I said, grinning. "I have a loving husband who takes care of all that stuff for me."

Bea laughed. "Okay, you two. Out. Call me tomorrow."

I untangled myself from Kane and reached over to hug her. Bea's arms came around me, and I held on for a beat longer than normal. She smelled of citrus and sunshine, and her soft embrace reminded me of my own mother, who lived in Idaho and was planning to visit after our daughter was born. It was nice to have a mother figure. Though I had to admit, Bea was just about the complete opposite of my earth mom, who spent her days in jeans and T-shirts in her shed, mixing healing herbs. Bea wore silk blouses and linen pants and looked like she belonged on her front porch, sipping mint juleps.

But looks were deceiving. Bea owned a new age shop in

the French Quarter, and when she wasn't working, she was often helping me or one of the other coven witches deal with any number of evil forces that seemed to be drawn to the Crescent City.

"Thanks, Bea," I said. "Let us know if Maximus has heard anything."

"Tomorrow," she said, her eyes twinkling with mischief. "I think you're not the only ones who might be having an early night."

CHAPTER 7

"Well. Sounds like age hasn't caught up to Bea and Maximus," I said as Kane drove us home.

He groaned. "That is not an image I need in my head the next time he's giving me an order."

I laughed. "No? I guess not."

"How are you doing, love?" His tone was soft and full of concern, matching the love that was streaming off him and wrapping around me like a blanket. He reached out and put his hand on my leg, squeezing gently.

"Better now that it's just us." I placed my hand over his, just for the connection. "I'm not sure I'm ready for this."

He turned the corner and pulled the car to a stop in front of the shotgun double we shared. "Don't worry. You have a whole team behind you. We'll find Harper, and your days will go back to prepping the nursery and helping Kat and Pyper with wedding preparations."

I sucked in a fortifying breath and shook my head. "That's not exactly what I meant."

His dark eyes flashed with concern. But instead of asking further questions, he said, "Hold that thought. This calls for ice cream, air-conditioning, and a neck rub."

I chuckled as he slipped out of the car and hurried over to my side to help me out. Sweat had soaked right through the back of my tank top, and the one thing I wanted more than anything in the world was a shower. The hours spent in lockup at the council, along with the late-August humidity, had left me sticky and completely worn down. The food and lemonade had helped somewhat, but I wasn't going to feel human again until I washed the day away.

Kane led me inside. Duke, the golden retriever ghost dog, met us at the door, his tail wagging and his tongue hanging out.

I smiled down at him. "Hey, boy. You haven't seen Flame, have you?"

The dog wagged his tail harder and turned around, leading us into the kitchen. Kane and I glanced at each other.

"You don't think that fire-breathing dog actually ended up back here, do you?" Kane said.

"No. How would she get over the bridge?" Still, we followed Duke into the kitchen, where he promptly sat in front of the back door as if waiting to go out. Since he was a ghost dog, if he wanted to enjoy the great outdoors, a door wasn't going to hinder him. I opened the back door and let out a small gasp as I recognized the small ball of fluff curled up in the shade under the small table we had out there.

The dog's head jerked up, and Flame let out a small bark as she darted into the house and ran for the water dish I'd left out earlier in the day. After lapping up some water, she trotted back over to me and collapsed at my feet.

Kane let out a sigh. "I guess that means we have a houseguest for the time being."

Holding on to the edge of the counter with one hand, I bent down and scooped her up with the other. She looked at me with weary eyes, yawned widely, and then tucked her head against my chest. "I think you might be right."

After rummaging around in the fridge for some leftover chicken breast, I made her a bowl of chicken and rice and set her down on the floor. She gobbled up her dinner in less than a minute and then just lay down on the tile floor and closed her eyes. In seconds, she was snoring.

"At least she isn't breathing fire," I whispered to Kane.

"That's something." He stared at the tiny brown dog. "How do you think she got here?"

"Who knows? Maybe Mati and Vaughn found her and brought her over."

"And just dumped her in the backyard without any water or food on an insufferable day in August?" he asked.

I had to admit it seemed unlikely, but I pulled out my cell phone and sent Mati a text to find out. Mati immediately texted back that she hadn't seen Flame since we'd been at her apartment earlier in the day. "It wasn't Mati and Vaughn. Maybe it was magic," I said with a yawn, my eyes watering with the effort of staying awake. "I don't know, but right now, I'm not sure I care. I need a shower and a nap."

"Nap?" Kane eyed the clock on the wall. "It's after eight

already. I think maybe you might just want to call it a night."

That was tempting, but... "Shower first." Then I grabbed his hand and led him into the master bedroom. "I might need someone to wash my back."

"You're sure?" he asked, already tugging his shirt off. The hint of the desire that had sparked between us earlier in the day came roaring back, and suddenly I wasn't quite as tired as I'd been a few moments before.

I chuckled. "I'm sure."

Kane disappeared into the bathroom, and before I could even kick my shoes off, I heard the water rush through the pipes and the spray of the shower. Then my husband was back, still wearing those low-slung jeans and looking sexier than ever. He knelt before me, gently slipping my shoes off and then reaching up to peel my pants off me. I sat on the edge of the bed, watching as his hands glided over my smooth skin, and wondered what I'd ever done to deserve him. He was everything I'd ever wanted—kind, gentle, loving, honorable, and a total badass when fighting evil. And hot. Pure man-candy. How we'd ended up together, I'd never fully understand, but I knew that I loved him more and more with each passing day. And I wouldn't trade a moment of this life even if it meant we never got another moment's peace.

"Your skin is so soft, Jade," Kane whispered and slid his hand up my inner thighs, parting them gently to make room for him to slip between them. His hands kept roaming upward, over my hips to my waist and then under my tank top, still moving up, up, up until he pulled the garment over my head, leaving me in just my red bra and panties.

My skin started to tingle all over, and I lay back on the bed, inviting him to explore anywhere he wanted.

"Goddess above, Jade. You just get lovelier every day." He reached down, his hands cupping my breasts while both thumbs gently stroked my nipples, turning them hard instantly.

I sucked in a sharp breath, staring up at his hard body, my fingers aching to touch him. "Come down here," I said, tugging on a loop of his jeans.

He chuckled softly. "Nope. We have a shower to take. Remember?"

I let out a small frustrated groan. Who cared about a shower when he'd just lit my body on fire? "If you lie down on this bed, I'll make it worth your while."

"Trust me, love. You want what I'm offering." He tugged on my hands, pulling me to my feet. Then he turned and led me into the bathroom. After divesting us both of the rest of our clothes, he opened the shower door and waved me in.

The lukewarm water hit my bare skin and I let out a sigh of pleasure. He was right. This was exactly what I needed.

Or at least it was what I *thought* I needed until his arms came around me from behind and his lips brushed over the back of my neck.

"That feels really good," I whispered.

"This is going to feel a hell of a lot better." His hands moved from my hips, one of them coming up to cup my breast while the other moved lower, dipping between my legs.

If Kane hadn't been an incubus, things might have been moving a little too quickly, but his desire was clinging to my skin, and because of our connection, I could feel exactly how much he wanted me. His passion lit a fire in me that made my knees weak.

He was a starving man who wanted me more now than he had when we'd first gotten together. And there was an urgency to his need that was no doubt fueled by the day's events, by his wondering when and if he was going to see his wife again.

"Kane," I said, leaning back against his chest and reaching one arm up and twining my fingers into his dark hair.

"Jade," he said, his voice husky. "You're so lush, so gorgeous. I can't keep my hands off you."

"No need to try," I said, breathless as he pressed his thumb against that bundle of nerves, which had me moaning my approval.

He continued to stroke me, whispering his love and affection as the water sluiced over us. Time seemed to stand still. Nothing else mattered except that moment as my husband loved me, as I filled up on the pleasure he brought me.

Trailing hot kisses down my neck, he moved on to my shoulder, and when my gasps became louder and shorter, he increased the pressure on my most sensitive spot, pinched my nipple with his other hand, and bit down on the nape of my neck.

Everything inside me tightened, the orgasm taking me so hard that lightning bolts exploded behind my eyes. My breath got caught in my throat, and my entire body shuddered with wave after wave of delicious release. Kane's arm tightened around my rib cage, holding me steady in case my legs failed to keep me upright. I was pure liquid in his arms, trembling with sweet, glorious pleasure.

"That's my girl," he whispered, gently running a washcloth over my back, my breasts, and my belly. I tried to turn to him, but he stilled me. "Let me do this first."

"But Kane. It's your turn," I said, my eyes closed as I reveled in his touch. What had I ever done to deserve this glorious, giving man?

"Soon, love. Let me take my time lathering you up. Then we'll move to the bed, where it's a little safer for you and the peanut."

I turned and gently took the soap from him. "Only if I get to return the favor."

"Jade, I— Oh God." His eyes closed as I wrapped my hand around his thick shaft, stroking him until he moaned. "This isn't... Christ."

He gently grabbed my wrist, stopping me, flipped the water off, and then hauled me into his arms and carried me to the bed.

After he set me down, his dark eyes shone with pure heat as he said, "On your knees."

Anticipation made me tremble as I grabbed the pillow to support my baby bump and crawled up to kneel on the bed.

Before I could even look back, Kane's hands grabbed my hips and he pressed himself to my opening, stopping just long enough to ask, "Are you ready?"

I nodded and let out a cry of pleasure as he plunged into me.

CHAPTER 8

"Well, someone looks happy," Pyper called from behind the counter. "I guess the black lace did its job."

"Waste of money. Never even took it out of the shopping bag," I said, walking toward the counter with Flame in tow.

Pyper raised her eyebrows. "You know I'm not supposed to let dogs in here, right?"

I snatched Flame up into my arms and gave Pyper a pained smile. "I know. I'm sorry. I couldn't leave her at the house. She already left a burn mark on the hardwood when Kane walked up behind her and startled her. I'm afraid she'll burn the house down, and it's too hot to leave her outside."

"Fine. Just keep her off the floor. Want something?"

"Decaf London Fog and a cinnamon scone, please." I grinned at her. "You're the best."

"I know," she said and eyed me again. "Did you have a good evening? You look positively shiny today."

"Very good." I glanced away, knowing by the heat in my cheeks that I was blushing furiously.

"Interesting. Guess the hubby needed a little intimacy after your time in the slammer." She winked, pulled a cinnamon scone out of the case, and placed it in the toaster.

"You, on the other hand, look like you barely slept." I eyed her messy ponytail and noted that while she was wearing a satisfied smile, her eyes were tinged red and slightly glassy. "Did that fiancé of yours keep you up all night or what?"

"It was ovulation day," she said just as Bo walked in from the back room.

"Oh geez," the teenager said with a groan. "Please, can you stop talking about your baby-making antics? It creeps me out."

His girlfriend Reagan, a pretty girl with dark hair and onyx eyes, was right behind him. She put her arm around her tall, lanky boyfriend and laughed. "Give her a break. She's trying to give you a niece or nephew to torture."

"That's perfectly fine," he said. "But I sure don't need to hear the details."

Pyper handed an apron to Bo and pointed to the specials board as she cackled.

I glanced up and covered a giggle. The chalk was moving across the board, drawing a picture of two eclairs in a compromising position. Next to the drawing, the words MAKING THE BEIGNETS appeared.

Bo rolled his eyes. "Thanks for the lesson, Ida May."

A light breeze rippled through the café, followed by the

bell jingling on the front door even though no one had walked in. It was Ida May's way of making her presence known.

"Keep an eye on these two, Ida May," Pyper told her ghost. "Make sure they don't get into any trouble."

I couldn't see her, but I could feel Ida May's joy and amusement. Her energy was light and full of love. Even though she was a ghost, she was living her best life.

"We're off to save the world," Pyper said, handing me my London Fog and toasted cinnamon scone in a paper bag.

"Again?" Bo and Reagan said at the same time.

"Always," Pyper and I responded. Then we looked at each other and laughed.

"Come on," she said, pulling her keys out of her pocket. "The VW is out back."

Still carrying Flame, I followed her through the back of the store and out to the parking spot where she kept her red VW Bug. She opened my door for me and held my tea and scone while I hauled myself into her car and put Flame on the floor near my feet. "If this vehicle gets any smaller, we're gonna need to trade it in for an SUV."

"That's funny. Julius and I were just talking about that. If we're lucky enough to end up with a baby on board, that's exactly what we'll be doing." She handed me my breakfast and hurried around to the driver's side. Once she was seat-belted in, she turned to me and asked, "Where to, boss? The university or back to the Witches' Council?"

The idea of going back to the Witches' Council so soon after being locked up made my stomach a little queasy. Or maybe that was because I hadn't actually eaten anything yet. Not to mention we couldn't take Flame there. I had no doubt that they'd confiscate her. Either way, the Witches' Council wasn't high on my list of places I wanted to go. "Head to Tulane. I'll text Mati and see if she can meet us there."

"You got it."

~

"JADE! PYPER!" Mati called from the steps outside the student union. She climbed to her feet, grabbed her backpack, and ran down to meet us.

I clutched Flame's leash, keeping her from getting near any of the other students. If one got in her way, who knew what would happen?

"Thank the gods you're okay," Mati said. "What happened yesterday?"

Pyper and I glanced at each other. "You didn't hear?"

"Well, just that you were hauled off to the Witches' Council." She shoved her phone into the pocket of her impossibly short shorts. She was wearing an off-the-shoulder white blouse with her bright red shorts and white wedges. If it hadn't been for the fierce scowl on her face, she looked like she could've been ready for the runway. "Those bastards. What crawled up their asses this time?"

"They wanted our help, and instead of asking for it, they coerced us instead," Pyper said.

"What dicks." She slung her backpack over her shoulder

and glanced at me. "I see Flame is with us. Did you find out how she ended up at your house?"

I shrugged. "No idea. She was just curled up at our back door when we got home."

Mati blinked. "That's strange. Isn't your gate locked? Did someone just put her back there?"

"Yes, it's locked, and it was still locked last night. Your guess is as good as mine. The way I see it, there are only two options—she's either a magical creature who somehow willed herself there, or someone put her there. A witch could've gotten in and out without any issues. But no way did Flame just run across the bridge and find her way back to our house without anyone noticing. So she's with me for the time being until I figure out what she is or why she's so important someone went out of their way to put her in my backyard."

Mati frowned as she studied Flame. "She looks so harmless."

"I know, right? Besides the sudden bursts of fire, she *is* mostly harmless." I shrugged. "She doesn't have an evil vibe. Maybe later today I'll take her by Bea's and see if she has any ideas."

"That sounds like a good idea," Mati said. "Are we ready to go? The sorority house is over on Broadway. Usually I just walk. Is that going to work, or do we need to find the car?"

"I'm good." I'd opted to wear a cotton baby doll dress and tennis shoes. As far as I was concerned, I was better prepared than both of them. Mati had on heels, and Pyper was wearing flip-flops with zero support and a black jumper that was likely to cause heatstroke. Though I had to admit that "good" might have been overstating things a bit. The late-summer heat was brutal, and I was already so hot that my dress was sticking to my skin.

"Here." Mati handed me a bottle of water and I nearly laughed as I took it and gulped down a sip. The cold water was welcome to my already overheated system.

"Thanks." I handed it to Pyper, who tipped the bottle to her lips and downed half the liquid.

"Is it really hot out here or is it just me?" she asked, wiping her forehead with the back of her hand.

"It's Hades hot," I said. "Come on. The sooner we get there, the sooner we'll have air-conditioning."

"This way." Mati took off down the street with Pyper and me right behind her.

The walk wasn't that far, but the humidity had done a number on all of us by the time we reached the white Victorian. The Greek letters KΩ were placed between the dormers just below the roofline.

"Looks like we made it," I said, lifting my long strawberry blond hair off the back of my neck and coiling it into a bun.

"I feel like I've been roasting on the devil's barbeque," Pyper complained. Her face was bright red, and the top of her black jumper was clinging to her skin.

"Come on." I grabbed her hand and hauled her under a large magnolia tree. "Why are you wearing black anyway? Are you crazy?"

"It's laundry day," she said simply.

"Man, I feel you," Mati said. "That's why I'm wearing these shorts. I didn't realize they were half an inch from showing my ass cheeks when I bought them."

"Girl, you look amazing. Wear those shorts as often as possible until your ass grows out of them. If I still had your assets, I'd be rocking those twice a week." Pyper glanced at me. "To be twenty-one again, right?"

I just laughed and shook my head. "You have the assets to wear something like that now, Pyper."

"You really do," Mati said, eyeing Pyper's backside as we walked up the pathway to the front door.

"Stop," she said, a grin spreading over her face. "You're embarrassing me."

I rolled my eyes. Pyper was an ex-stripper who used to regularly wear only body paint during festivals. Now she was more likely to be found doing the painting rather than wearing it, but there was no way a little talk about her assets was embarrassing her.

Mati grabbed a large gold knocker and banged it against the dark walnut door. After a minute went by and we didn't hear anything inside, I pressed the doorbell. Music that sounded a lot like the *Bewitched* theme song played inside.

"That would get annoying quickly," Pyper said.

I laughed. "I love it. Do you think Kane would object if I changed our bell to something like that?"

"Probably." Pyper leaned to the left and let the sprinkler running on the side of the house douse her face with water. She wiped it away and added, "But if you ask him while wearing that black number, he probably won't care."

"Solid point," I said, nodding. It wasn't that Kane was

89

usually easily manipulated, it was just that when he was distracted, he was much more agreeable.

The door swung open, and a petite blonde clapped her hands together and nearly squealed when she spotted Mati. "Oh gosh! You're here! Yay!" She slipped her arm through Mati's and tugged her inside as she said, "You know you can just walk right in, don't you? You're part of the house now. Just because you don't live here doesn't mean this isn't your home too."

Mati glanced over her shoulder at us and jerked her head, indicating we were to follow.

Pyper didn't hesitate and let out a relieved sigh the moment the air-conditioning hit her. I tugged on Flame's leash and walked into the house. The Victorian was old with scuffed wood floors and a banister, which badly needed refinishing, leading to the second story, but the place was incredible. There were quality built-ins along the wall in the living room, large ten-foot-long windows overlooking the front yard, and gorgeous antique chandeliers in every room. I had no trouble seeing what it must've looked like a century ago.

"Listen, Cami," Mati said. "We're here to see the new recruits. The ones Harper brought in. Are they here?"

Her lips pursed as she glanced up the stairs. "They're here, but they haven't helped us with the autumn ball planning or the love spells we're casting for rush week. Honestly, I'm not even sure if they're Kappa Mu material."

Mati stepped back and blinked at the perky blonde. "Are you serious? You do know Harper went missing yesterday, right?"

She waved an unconcerned hand. "She's probably just getting a jump on her schoolwork. I'm sure she'll be here tonight for the sisterhood ceremony."

"No one has heard from her since she disappeared from the Witches' Council. I highly doubt she'll come here for a ceremony." Mati looked over Cami's head and gave me a can-you-believe-this look.

No, I couldn't. Cami was so flippant about the situation I was starting to wonder if she wasn't in on Harper's disappearance. Why else would she be acting so tone-deaf?

"The Witches' Council?" she asked, confused. "What are you talking about?"

I bit back an annoyed sigh. How was it possible a witch in New Orleans, especially one who was president of the college sorority for witches, could be so out of touch with what was going on in the community? This type of thing spread like wildfire. I hadn't told anyone in the coven about yesterday's events except Lucien, but I had no doubt that if I called any one of them they'd already have heard the rumors.

"The Witches' Council hauled Harper away from work yesterday," Mati said. "After an hour or so, she just disappeared from their custody. She wasn't released. Either the council is lying and they still have her, or she's MIA." She waved to me. "You know who Jade Calhoun is, right?"

Cami's eyes went wide as saucers as she stared at me. "White witch," she whispered.

"That's right. And coven leader of New Orleans. She and her friend Pyper have been ordered by the council to find Harper." Mati picked up a notebook near the house phone and flipped through the written messages. When she didn't see anything noteworthy, she put the pad back down. "So if anyone here knows anything at all, it's imperative that we speak to them. Harper hasn't made contact with you, has she?"

"Me?" Cami pressed a hand to her chest and took a step back. "No. Of course not." Then she frowned. "If Harper is a fugitive from the Witches' Council, she can't be part of Kappa Mu. We don't deal with rogues." She glanced toward the ceiling and bit her lip. "Her recruits are upstairs. If it turns out they have any part in this trouble, they'll have to go too."

Cami wasn't wrong in her assessment. If Harper and her friends were warring with the council, that was a liability the sorority couldn't handle. Maybe she was savvier than I'd given her credit for. College was pretty insular after all, especially when one had such a full plate.

"Cami," I said. "Do you have any idea who Harper was closest to? Someone she hung out with more than anyone else?"

Her brow furrowed as she considered the question. "I think the raven-haired one. Willow? Wilma?"

"Willa," Mati said. "Tall, athletic, brilliant green eyes."

"Yes! That one," Cami confirmed. "And she has a boyfriend I think. He's a music major. Plays the violin. First chair. I don't know his name."

"That's a start," I said and glanced over at Pyper. She had her head cocked to one side as if she were listening to something... or someone. "What is it?" I asked her.

"Not sure yet. There's a conversation about the ancient

ones, but I'm not quite following. Something about resurrection and the order of things."

Cami's frown deepened. "I don't hear anything."

"Pyper's a medium," I said. "She's listening in on ghosts."

The sorority president was silent for a long moment. Then she blurted, "Are you telling me there are ghost pervs watching us while we shower?"

"Probably," I said, unable to stop my laughter. "This is New Orleans after all. Almost every old home is visited by ghosts. It's just the way of things."

"That's not funny!" she cried. "How would you feel if a ghost was watching you?"

"Creeped out," I said honestly. "When I first moved here, I actually did have a ghost join me in the shower. He freaked me out so badly I fell and almost hit my head on the toilet. I could've knocked myself out and died. It wasn't pretty."

"How did you handle it?" she asked, her tone hushed.

"I smudged the place with sage."

"Did it work?"

I shook my head. "Not exactly. But that was a special case. Most of the time it does. If you're worried, go to Beatrice Kelton's shop, the Herbal Connection, in the French Quarter. She'll help you find the right herbs and spells to oust even the most persistent ghosts."

"Okay." She crossed her arms over her chest and glanced around, no doubt looking for any pervy ghosts.

"Pyper? Anything?" I asked.

She shook her head. "The voices stopped, and Tru says they've moved on for now." Tru was one of her spirit guides.

I nodded. "All right. Let's go talk to Willa and the others." I glanced at Cami. "Which room is it?"

"The one at the very end of the hall. You can't miss it."

"Got it." I took off up the stairs, Flame in my arms, Mati and Pyper behind me.

CHAPTER 9

*L*avender incense overwhelmed me as I stepped through the threshold of the bedroom door. I noted Willa instantly. She was folded into a wooden chair at the desk, her dark hair tied back in a loose ponytail. There was a mustard stain on her white off-the-shoulder T-shirt, and she was still wearing cotton pajama bottoms.

Her bright green gaze raked over me, and then she gasped and jumped up, her arms out as she said, "Peanut, there you are."

Flame started wiggling in my arms, desperate to get to Willa.

"Come here, sweetie. Oh, sweet demons, I'm so glad you're all right." She pulled Flame—err, Peanut—out of my arms and cuddled her close to her chest. "Where did you find her?" Willa asked me.

Not sure I wanted everyone to know the pup had

somehow magically ended up in my backyard, I went with the easiest explanation. "We were there when the council took Harper. After this one showed off her talents, I couldn't leave her there, so I took her home with me."

Willa let out a deep sigh of relief. "Thank you, thank you," she said, rubbing her cheek against the dog's fur. "You saved her."

I glanced at the other two women who were sitting on the bed and leaning against the wall. One was dark skinned with tight curls that had been dyed blond, while the other one was so fair her skin seemed almost translucent. They were both smiling at Willa and Peanut, clearly pleased at the development.

"I don't know if *saved* is the correct word," I said. "She seems to be able to handle herself. But I didn't want to risk her falling into the wrong hands. The mundane world would have no idea what to do with her."

"Well, thank you anyway." Willa held out a hand to me. "I'm Willa Hamilton, Harper's cousin."

Cousin? That was interesting. Was she the daughter of the aunt who lived in Salem? I shook her hand. "Jade Calhoun."

Willa gave me a brisk nod. "I've heard of you. You're the one who helped Conor Wells a few months ago."

"That was me, as well as Mati and some other friends." I gave her a warm smile, hoping to gain her trust before I revealed that I was supposed to be hunting her cousin.

She glanced nervously at the other two women and then back at me. "Do you know where she is? Harper, I mean?"

"I was hoping to ask you the same question." I took two

steps over to the bed and held my hand out to the dark-skinned woman. "Hi. I'm Jade."

"Mack." She shook my hand and then turned to the fair-skinned woman. "And this is Ellie."

"Hi, Ellie." I shook her hand too and then introduced Pyper.

After everyone was acquainted, I turned back to Willa expectantly. "Any idea of where Harper might be?"

Her eyes were sad as she just shook her head. "We've already checked everywhere we could think of. We don't know anything other than she just vanished into thin air."

Willa's energy had a hesitant feeling that made me feel like she was hiding something. I didn't think she was lying exactly, just more like holding back. Reading people without their permission wasn't something that I liked to do. In fact, usually I took pains to block out others' emotions. They were just too taxing, especially when they were bombarding me all the time. But the energy from all three of them was different than what I was used to. It was faint, barely there, yet it called to me the way another intuitive's energy always did.

"And you don't have any guesses on where to try next?" I asked, sending my emotional energy out, trying to read her response.

"None," Willa said. "Not unless she left New Orleans, which I doubt. She wouldn't have done that without Peanut." She stroked the dog's ears. "Want to come home with me, sweetheart? Diesel will be overjoyed for a playmate."

"Diesel?" I asked.

"That's Peanut's brother," Ellie interjected.

"The fire-breathing dog has a brother?" I asked, shocked. "There are more of them? How?"

Willa shrugged. "How are there dragons or witches or demons?"

That was a good question. "Mind telling me where you found the dogs? Are they dogs? I'm not really sure."

Willa laughed. "Yes, of course they are. There's a guy out in the bayou who breeds them. I think he must be some sort of witch, but I'm not really sure. My mom hooked us up with him when we got down here. She has connections all over the country."

"The one with a shop in Salem?" I asked.

"That's the one."

"Listen, Willa," Mati said, sitting down next to her. "I hope this isn't too personal, but your mom's a witch, right?"

"Yes." She chuckled softly. "What's personal about that?"

"But you aren't, are you?" Mati asked.

Willa stiffened, and her eyes darkened with annoyance. "No. I'm not a witch, but I have other abilities. Like I know that you and your incubus boyfriend filled the well last night, so to speak."

Mati just stared at her. Then she finally said, "That's true enough, but we do most nights." She shrugged as if the fact that some random person had intimate knowledge of her sex life didn't matter in the least. Maybe it didn't. Mati was a sex witch after all.

"And the one with the blue hair." Willa nodded to Pyper. "She's not a witch. In fact, she doesn't have any power at all. Her only skill is talking to dead people."

So Willa could sense other people's paranormal abilities. That was quite handy actually. "What about me?" I asked her. "You already know I'm a witch."

She gave me a flat stare. "You tried to read my energy to see if I was lying to you. How'd that go?"

My mouth fell open at her bluntness. But as the shock wore off, I just laughed. "Actually, not well. I'm sorry. I shouldn't have done that. Your emotional signature is unique, and that interests me. Now I know why."

Willa stood. "All I'm interested in is finding my cousin before it's too late. Are you here to help, or are you wasting my time?"

"Too late for what?" Pyper and I asked at the same time.

No one said anything as Willa stared at the floor, her head bowed.

"Willa?" I asked gently.

She raised her head and shook it. Silent tears were rolling down her face.

"You have to tell her," Mack said in almost a whisper. "It's what Harper wanted."

"Jade works for the council," Willa said, wiping angrily at her cheeks. "She's not who we thought she was."

So she'd heard that part, had she? Well, better that she knew the truth even if I didn't technically work for them. Pyper and I had been forced to do their bidding, and that would never sit right.

"Yes, she is," Ellie said, climbing off the bed and taking Willa's hand in her own. "She saved Conor, and she can save Harper too."

Dread coiled in the pit of my stomach. There'd been a

list of possible dragon leaders with my name circled. Harper had been arrested for trying to unleash the dragon. There was a fire-breathing dog that acted as more of a familiar. I'd been trying not to jump to conclusions, but the obvious was now staring me in the face.

"Harper is in danger of becoming a dragon, and that's why everyone wants me to find her, is that it?" I asked. "Everyone is hoping I can save her and the city?"

The look on Willa's face told me I'd hit the nail smack on the head.

"Tell me everything."

Willa reached into a purse that was sitting on the desk and pulled out a piece of paper. It was a short list of names. "These are our cousins from my mother's oldest sister. They all went missing in the past two months."

"What?" Mati got up from the chair and started pacing the room. "How? What happened?"

I moved to take Mati's place, grateful to get off my feet, and grabbed a pen out of my own bag, staring expectantly at Willa, waiting for her to answer.

She swallowed and looked at Mack and Ellie pleadingly.

Mack climbed off the bed and moved to Willa's side. Taking her hand, she said, "They're all older than us. Out of college and all living in separate towns. Lacy went missing first, but it took a while for anyone to notice because she travels a lot. They thought she was on a business trip. But two weeks later, Bree disappeared on her way to a yoga class, and three days after that, Janice disappeared on her way to work. All three are missing without a trace. No one knows anything."

My heart sped up and a sense of urgency flared to life in my chest. "Did anyone do a finding spell?"

Willa nodded.

"What happened?"

"My aunt showed up in the circle." Willa clutched the paper, crinkling it. "She passed ten years ago after a spell backfired."

"She appeared as a ghost then?" Pyper asked.

Willa nodded. "She said she feared this would happen. That when they found out, they'd eliminate us. She told Harper and me to find you. That you were the only one who could protect us. But now…" She shook her head. "Just tell me now. Are you going to turn us in to the council?"

"Why would I do that?" I asked, stunned.

"Because, Jade," Mack said, standing up straighter. "We're the last—"

"No, Mack!" Willa said, her expression alarmed. "Don't say anything."

"Willa," Mack said, her voice full of fatigue, "we're out of options. Who else is going to help us? What are Ellie and I going to do when you're next and then they come for us?"

Willa buried her face in her hands.

"Come for you two as well?" I asked. "Are you all related?"

Mack and Ellie nodded.

Ellie gave me a weak smile and added, "We're distant cousins, but still cousins of the same bloodline. We've been close our entire lives."

"Dammit, Ellie," Willa said, though the fight had gone out of her. She turned and stared me in the eye. "We are the last descendants of the Viscount Dragons. Two months ago, when Conor Wells turned into a dragon, our gifts started to manifest. It was slow at first. We didn't even know it was happening. But now there's no questioning it." She closed her eyes for a moment as if she was concentrating, and then her skin took on an orange glow. Then she put Peanut on the ground and raised her hands palms up. Fire flickered over her scaly palms as a flame danced in her eyes. In the next moment the magic vanished, and she was a normal college girl once more.

"Whoa," I said, still trying to process what I'd seen. She'd had an inner fire, dragon scales similar to Conor's on her arms, and she was able to wield the fire with perfect precision. But she hadn't turned into a dragon like Conor had. Whatever was going on, it wasn't the same as when a dragon soul had taken over Conor's body.

Willa reached down, picked up Peanut, and started to pet her ears again. The action seemed to calm her as the strain eased from her face. "As you can see, there's no denying that my aunt was right. We definitely have dragon gifts."

"Holy hell," I breathed and looked over at Mati.

Her expression was grim, but she didn't say anything. I think we were both remembering the epic takedown of Conor when he'd turned into a full-fledged dragon.

I cleared my throat and asked, "Are these... gifts new?"

All three of the cousins nodded.

"And, um, are they controllable? I mean, do they just manifest, or do you wield them like a witch would her own magic?" I held my breath. If they were uncontrollable, these women were a serious threat to all of us.

"They are absolutely controllable," Willa said. "No one here is possessed like Conor. We are not a danger to society. We're the ones in danger. We're the ones going missing, and we have no idea why."

I certainly did. There were only two possible reasons they were being targeted; either someone was trying to eliminate them, or they were trying to use them. And now I had a choice to make—go along with the council and bring them in or try to save these women from whatever was out there waiting for them.

My choice was already made.

I leaned forward, my hands clasped together as I stared at Pyper, silent communication passing between us. She gave me a curt nod. I knew she'd agree. I flashed her a quick smile and then said, "Ladies, I promise you, you can trust us. Harper was right. I'll do everything in my power to help you."

"You will?" Willa asked, blinking in surprise.

"You're damned straight I will. Now start at the beginning. I need to know everything."

CHAPTER 10

$\mathcal{W}$illa and her cousins looked at each other, and then all three turned to me with a blank stare.

"What?" I asked.

"We've already told you everything we know," Mack said.

"But you said you have dragon-blood heritage. Start there."

Again they didn't say anything and just shook their heads.

"You don't know who your ancestor is?" I asked, filling in the blanks.

"Our aunt just said he was a descendant from our grandmother's side of the family, but that's all we know," Ellie said. "This is all really new. Can you imagine finding out you have these strange powers and no idea where they came from?"

"Yes," Pyper said. "I wasn't always a medium."

"Then you know how strange it is," Mack said with a short nod. "Our aunt is a witch, but no one else in the family is, so we thought maybe we were coming into some late powers or something. But we only control fire. Nothing else. Willa has some sort of intuition, but she's always had that."

I sucked in a sharp breath. "Okay then. We need to find someone who knows dragon lore." I glanced at Mati. "Any ideas?"

She shook her head. "I'd come to you or the council... but they appear to be out of the question. If they're behind the disappearances, it wouldn't be good to go tipping them off."

Mati was right. Giving them any reason to suspect I was helping the women would put us all in danger. But I had a secret weapon. There was a ghost at the council who'd taken a liking to me. With Pyper's help, we might be able to contact her again.

I kept that to myself and said, "Anyone else?"

"The breeder," Willa said, eyeing Peanut. "He said the puppies would be perfect for people like us. I didn't know what he meant at the time. But... well, I think he knew what we were, otherwise why would he give us fire-breathing dogs?"

It was a start. "Address?"

She found it in her address book and handed it over. After jotting it down, I stood.

"Okay, if you hear anything else or think of something I need to know, don't hesitate to call." I dug around in my bag, found a card, and handed it to her, then signaled to Pyper. "Ready?"

"Ready," she said.

I hugged each of the young women, trying my best to send positive energy their way. They were going to need it. To Willa I said, "I'm going to want your cousins' information. The ones who went missing. I'll put my second in charge of seeing if he can track anything down on them. Their names, addresses, places of work. Anything else relevant. Okay?"

"Okay," she said, her voice a little shaky.

"Don't worry. I'm not going to stop until we find Harper and figure this out, all right? I promise."

"Thank you," she whispered in my ear, holding on tight. Her fear suddenly burst through her hardened exterior, and my entire body started to ache for the scared young woman in front of me. It was then that my promises to them were solidified. They hadn't asked for any of this, and they sure as hell weren't going to pay the price for something they had no control over.

"Mati," I said after I let Willa go, "will you walk us out?"

"Sure."

The three of us were silent as we made our way down the grand old staircase. Once we were outside, I turned to Mati and said, "Keep a sharp eye on them, okay? If you think we need backup, let me know and I'll get my coven witches to help."

"You got it." Her expression was troubled. After taking a deep breath, she said, "Dragons? Is this real?"

"You saw what I did. What do you think?"

She pressed her lips together and rubbed the back of her neck. "I think this world just keeps getting crazier and crazier."

I laughed. "No doubt. But at least they aren't demons, right?"

She returned my smile with a slight grimace. "Careful. You wouldn't want to jinx it."

"Fair enough." I nodded to the house. "Now go inside and plan your parties like nothing's amiss. I don't want to draw any attention to Harper's cousins."

She sucked in a deep breath as if fortifying herself, nodded, and walked back inside.

Pyper glanced at me. "We're headed to the bayou, aren't we?"

I eyed her black outfit. "Want to change first?"

"Yes, but it's laundry day, remember?" She waved a hand. "Never mind. Let's just go. I'm dying to hear all about how this swamp witch created dragon puppies."

"Are you sure we're going the right way?" Pyper asked, stopping at the entrance of an old wooden bridge. "You think we can make it over that rickety thing without ending up in the bayou?"

I leaned forward, peering out the windshield. There was obvious rot on the edge of some of the boards closest to us, and the entire thing appeared to be tilting to the right. "There's only one way to find out."

"What's that? Some sort of spell?" Pyper asked.

If only I had something up my sleeve. I shook my head, opened the door, and hauled myself out of the car. The buzz of swamp bugs was thick in the air, and the humidity was so oppressive it was hard to get enough oxygen in my lungs. After taking a moment to catch my breath, I walked over to the bridge and—

"Jade, what are you doing?" Pyper asked from right behind me.

My heart jumped into my throat as she startled me. "Hell, Pyper. Don't do that."

She shook her head. "What were you going to do? Walk over it and see if it crumbled?"

"No." I rolled my eyes and moved to the edge, glancing down at the piers. They were evenly spaced and plenty thick. That was a good sign.

"Uh, Jade," Pyper said, her tone hesitant.

"Hold on. I'm just going to give it a jolt of magic and then—"

"There's an alligator behind you," she hissed.

Fear crawled down my spine. Magic instantly pooled in my palms as I slowly turned around to find a giant fourteen-foot gator, his jaws open wide as if he were going to swallow me whole. I didn't dare move another inch. Alligators didn't see all that well and often struck based on movement alone. My heart pounded against my rib cage. Would my magic be enough to stop him if he attacked? I had no idea. Their leather hides were thick, and it was notoriously hard to kill one.

But luckily I didn't need to find out. The gator closed his

giant mouth and then ambled across the bridge as if he was just on his midmorning stroll.

"Holy shit," Pyper said, grabbing my hand and pulling me back into the car. Once she was behind the wheel, she said, "That's enough of the great outdoors."

"So what? We're just going to turn around and go home?" I asked her.

"Nope. We're following that gator. Did you see how the bridge didn't even flex? Do you know how much a giant alligator weighs?"

"No. Never had a reason to find out... thank the gods."

"About a thousand pounds. I think the bridge is fine." Without another word, she put her car into gear and shot across the bridge. The structure was as solid as they come.

I glanced back at it, my eyes narrowed. The boards still looked rotted, and now it appeared to be leaning the other direction, and I had a feeling someone had gone through a lot of trouble to make the bridge look as unsafe as possible.

Pyper steered her car around a curve in the road, bringing us to an old shack that looked roughly the same as the bridge. It was a small cottage that sat right on the edge of the bayou and had a rusted old airboat tied to a dock. To the left was a large barn and a fenced area that contained a chicken coop and fancy colorful chickens pecking at the ground.

We both climbed out of the red Beetle and glanced around.

The front door opened, and a tall, dark-skinned man strode out, a rifle slung over one shoulder and a mug in his hand. "You lost?"

"I don't think so," I said, strolling over to his porch. "We're looking for a breeder of sorts. Our friend Willa pointed us in your direction. She and her cousin Harper—"

"I know who Willa and Harper are," he said, his voice gruff. "What do you want?"

Pyper and I glanced at each other. He wasn't at all welcoming, though few who lived deep in the bayou were. They didn't take kindly to strangers showing up out of the blue. His energy was closed off to me, as if he was shielding it. Which was probably a good thing. If my energy invaded his, there was no telling how he'd handle it. He wasn't exactly Mr. Friendly. I cleared my throat. "I'm Jade Calhoun, the coven—"

"Coven leader of New Orleans. And Betty Boop over there is a medium who owns a coffee shop on Bourbon. You're also working for the council, and that's all I need to know about you. Now go before I unleash Trevor."

"Trevor?" Pyper asked.

"My swamp dog. He doesn't take kindly to trespassers."

"We're not working for the council," I blurted as he turned his back to us.

"You're lying, Ms. Calhoun. I know everything that goes on in that hellhole. As of yesterday, you work for them whether you like it or not." He kept walking toward the barn, his steps brisk.

"Wait!" I called after him. "You don't understand. We were coerced into working for the council, and right now our biggest priority is finding Harper to make sure she's safe and protecting her cousins from being abducted."

He paused for a few beats. Then he turned around and

glared at me. "Working for the council puts you on the wrong side of history."

"I strongly suspect that you are correct, sir, but at the moment, it's either tell them I'll work for them or they're going to incarcerate Pyper and me on trumped-up charges. The best thing I can do for everyone involved is cooperate with them—"

Fire flashed in his eyes, and he snarled as he started to speak.

I held up my hand and raised my voice as I continued, "If they think we're cooperating, we're free to help Harper and her cousins. If it turns out that Harper did nothing wrong, I will do everything in my power to help her and her missing cousins."

"What she said." Pyper jerked a thumb at me. "No one controls Jade, or me for that matter. And if you know so much about the council, you know that Jade has no reason to be loyal to them."

We both stared him down.

He glared back. Finally he let out a put-upon sigh and walked over to the barn. "Hurry up then. I don't have all day."

Without hesitation, we moved as fast as we could to keep up with him. But in my condition, fast was relative. By the time I crossed the dirt lot, my head was starting to spin from the heat and lack of hydration.

"Here." Pyper produced a bottle of water from her purse and handed it to me.

I nearly cried with relief. My bag was still in her car where I'd left it. "Do you have a snack in there too?"

She rolled her eyes but produced a small package of cashews and handed those over as well.

"You're a lifesaver."

"I know." She quickly tied her hair up to get it off her neck and followed the man into the barn.

I shoved the nuts into my dress pocket, took a few gulps of water, and followed.

Inside, the barn was impeccable. The floor had been swept clean, and to the right was a wall full of food and supplies for the animals. To the left there were a dozen large, empty kennels.

"Where are the animals?" I asked, starting to wonder if we'd been led into a hinky situation. The cages were certainly large enough to hold humans as long as they were sitting down. My imagination started to run wild as magic pooled at my palms, my unease putting me on high alert.

"Put your magic away, white witch!" the man ordered, his voice harsh. "Do it now, or this visit is over."

"Where are the animals?" I asked again, ignoring his demand.

"Jade—" Pyper started, but I cut her off.

"We aren't easy marks if that's what you're thinking. You can't just lead us in here and pretend—"

"Jade!" Pyper grabbed my arm and pointed to an adjacent room. The door was open, and half a dozen dogs were lounging around. Two of them were sitting in small kiddie pools while the other four sat right in front of their own personal oscillating fans with their tongues lolling out in pure doggie pleasure.

"Oh." My magic vanished instantly. I gave the man an

apologetic smile. "Sorry about that. In my line of work, things can get ugly fast. I suppose I'm a little on edge."

"You do not use magic in here ever," he barked. "It will disrupt the spells already in place that keep the animals... in their best breeding form."

I glanced at the six dogs. Two were schnauzers, two were bulldogs, and the last two were white and fluffy... Maltese perhaps. "You've spelled them to, ah, get it on?"

"What?" He shook his head. "No. Gods above, woman. What is wrong with you?" He cracked a smile, the first one we'd seen since braving his front door. "They don't need any encouragement from me. The spells enhance their gifts and pass them down to their litters."

"Um," Pyper said. "I'm sorry, but we didn't get your name."

He turned his gaze on her, and for a moment I thought he was going to ignore her statement. But then he gave her a short nod. "Elijah."

"Nice to meet you Mr. Elijah," Pyper said. "If you don't mind, can I ask why you're breeding magical beings?"

His dark eyes flickered with surprise. "Because dragons need an energy outlet or else they can lose control of their fire. They are the dragons' familiars."

"So it's true what Willa and the others said then." I walked over to the open door and gazed at the seemingly normal dogs. "Harper and her cousins are turning into dragons?"

He moved to the open door and stood next to me. "What do you know about dragons, Ms. Calhoun?"

I glanced at his weathered face. "Not much. Just that

they used to be the protectors of angels and a few hundred years ago they were wiped out in an epic war... or at least everyone thought they had been until that dragon soul found a way into Conor Wells's body."

"That's right." He wandered into the room and sat next to one of the fluffy white dogs. The pup pawed at his leg and he reached down, picking it up and positioning it in his lap. "And as you know, the council will do everything in their power to annihilate the dragons. That puts Harper and her family at risk, as well as any other remaining humans with dragon lineage."

"There are more?" Pyper asked, now standing next to me and leaning against the doorframe.

"Of course there are more," he said impatiently.

"If that's true, then how have they been hidden all this time?" I couldn't make sense of his statement, and if I hadn't seen Willa's power with my own two eyes, I'd have been questioning if the guy was for real.

"Because, Jade Calhoun, when your friend succumbed to the dragon earlier this summer, he called them home. Dragons all around the country are awakening, and the council will do everything in their power to neutralize them."

I sucked in a sharp breath. "Called them home? What does that mean?"

"He woke their inner dragons. Now that the council has that dragon soul trapped and stashed away, they won't have a leader. One of the awakened will rise to power, and dragons will once again walk among us."

"And you're helping them?" I asked, although I already knew the answer. He *was* breeding familiars for them.

His lips curved into a small smile. "I think that's obvious."

"Why?" I had to know his reasons. Did he want to control them? Was he warring with the council? Did he have angel connections? Dragons had once been angel protectors after all.

He tilted his head to the side and studied me. "Why do you want to help?"

"I don't have a choice," I said with a shrug.

"That's not the entire truth."

He was right, of course. I would help Harper and her friends even if the council hadn't forced my hand.

"She does it because she can't help herself," Pyper said. "If someone is in trouble, she jumps in with both feet as if she has some sort of obligation."

"As if you don't do the same thing," I said hotly.

She just laughed. "Fair enough. But I think I picked up that habit from you. There's something deeply satisfying about helping someone who desperately needs it."

"There you go," Elijah said. "I do it because I can and if I don't, no one else will."

"There are others who breed familiars," I pointed out.

He ran a hand over his bald head. "That's true. But none as experienced as me and none who would deal with dragons."

"You've bred other familiars?" Pyper asked.

He nodded, studying her. "You're easy. A cat would be perfect for you."

"No argument there," she said with a chuckle.

His gaze focused on me, and it took him a little longer, but finally he said, "A dog. Probably a golden retriever."

I couldn't help it. I laughed as I thought of Duke, my ghost dog, and said, "That makes sense. I kind of already have one."

We followed him out of the barn into the clearing. Before we turned to go, he handed me a card with just a phone number on it. "If you run into any dragons who need a familiar, you send them my way. Discreetly, you understand?"

"Got it," I said and held out my hand to him. "Thank you, Elijah. You've been very helpful."

He gripped my hand with his, a magical spark crackling over our hands, indicating he was a very powerful witch. We gazed at each other with mutual respect until he said, "Don't betray me or those girls. If the council finds out we've had this conversation, it will not end well."

"You have my word," I said. "And Pyper's too."

My friend nodded, her bright blue eyes locked on Elijah's.

The older man blew out a breath. "Be careful. You've landed yourself in the middle of a shit storm with ruthless players on all sides."

I swallowed the nervousness rising up in the back of my throat and forced out, "This isn't my first rodeo."

His gaze flickered down to my swollen belly, but he didn't say anything. Instead, he led the way to Pyper's car, which was parked on the other side of the house. As soon as we turned the corner, Pyper and I came to a dead stop as we spotted the giant fourteen-foot gator draped over the hood of her car.

Elijah just laughed. "I see Trevor is a fan of the Beetle."

"Trevor? Your *swamp dog*?" I asked, remembering his earlier comment.

"Yep. He patrols the property. Only lets those he deems worthy over the bridge." The older man's eyes glittered as he glanced down at me. "Or the ones I tell him to let through."

So… he'd known all along that Pyper and I were on that bridge. We'd have never been let through if he hadn't wanted us to find him. "Trevor is your familiar, isn't he?"

His smile broadened, but he didn't answer. Instead, Elijah snapped his fingers and the gator slowly started to make his way off Pyper's car.

"Oh geez." Pyper winced. "He's going to leave scratches, isn't he?"

"Nah," Elijah said. "He's gentle."

Sure enough, the gator crawled off the car without leaving a mark and rambled over to Elijah, stopping just beside him. Both of them stared at us, and I could've sworn they were both wearing the same grim expression.

"Be careful, Jade Calhoun. You too, Pyper Rayne," Elijah said, his voice low and full of urgency. "Those women are depending on you."

"We'll find them," I promised and prayed we didn't let any of them down.

CHAPTER 11

$\mathcal{M}$y phone buzzed with incoming texts not long after we left the bayou. Pyper had just turned onto a paved two-lane road that would take us back to the city as I read the multiple messages from Lucien.

"Oh, son of... Dammit." I turned to Pyper. "We're late for our lunch with Kat. Very late."

She glanced at the clock on the dash and groaned. "Oh no. She's never going to forgive us."

"Not if she waited for us to eat, she won't." I quickly searched for my best friend's name and hit Call. It didn't even ring on my end before she answered.

"Jade, where the hell are you two? I've been here for an hour already. Your sushi rolls are getting soggy."

At least she'd ordered. The knowledge did little to ease my guilt. The truth was, once we'd landed at Elijah's place, I'd forgotten we had lunch plans. "I'm so sorry, Kat. We were running down a lead for our new assignment, and we ended up in the bayou, waiting for an alligator to surrender Pyper's car before we could come meet you."

"An alligator? What are you going on about? Is this just another way to get out of the wedding shower planning?"

I bit my lower lip. The week before, I'd called in "pregnant" when I was supposed to help her with her dried herb candles that invited health, love, and friendship. One of the herbs had been making me nauseated. She hadn't quite believed me. My excuse had been half true. The herb did make my stomach turn, but only if I had to ingest it. Since there wasn't supposed to be any sampling, I should've been fine. It was just that I'd been exhausted, and when Kane had offered a foot massage, I'd caved and bailed on the ninety-minute planning session.

"I swear it isn't. We're on our way now. We should be there in ten minutes."

"A lot of good that will do," she muttered.

Guilt started to take over, and my cheeks flushed. Thank goodness she couldn't see me, because she'd known me long enough that there would be no mistaking what my flush meant. "I really am sorry, Kat. We'll be right there."

"Fine. Just hurry."

PYPER and I parked in a nearby lot and hurried to the sushi place in the CBD. The restaurant was just on the other side of Canal Street but was just enough off the beaten path that it was more of a local's place that wasn't filled with a lot of tourists.

Kat was sitting by the window, drumming her fingernails on the table while she scrolled through her phone.

"We're here," I said, out of breath from the brisk walk. After I took a seat across from her, I added, "Sorry again."

"Yeah. Sorry about that, Kat." Pyper sat between us and downed a glass of water.

"I have to leave in five minutes." Kat shook her head, making her red curls fall over one eye. "Since we didn't have time to discuss the details that still need to be taken care of, I just made you both lists. Is that all right? Or do you just want me to take care of everything?"

I'd expected her to be angry, instead she just sounded a little dejected. I reached across the table and placed my hand over hers. A jolt of her nervous energy hit me, followed by a faint trace of sadness. "What's wrong, Kat?" I asked. "Is it because we were late? Or is there something else worrying you?"

She let out a small laugh and pulled her hand back. "I really hate that you can do that. You know that, right?"

"No, you don't." I flashed her a knowing smile. "You secretly love that you can't keep things hidden from me. It forces you to talk about whatever it is that's bothering you. Now which is it? Are you upset we were late and not focused on your big day, or is it something else?"

Kat moved her hand and rested it at the base of her throat. "I don't know. I think I'm just nervous and wanted some girl time to relax, and then…"

"We didn't show," Pyper said and stuffed a rainbow roll in her mouth.

"Something like that." Kat glanced away, clearly still out of sorts.

"Hand over the lists," I said. "Pyper and I've got this."

Pyper nodded and used her chopsticks to stab a piece of tuna sashimi.

Kat slid a short list of to-do items to us. Each errand had detailed notes such as *double-check the wine is vintage 1997 or 1999, but not 1998* and *make sure the filling is cappuccino, not espresso.*

"These are a piece of cake," I said. "We'll tackle most of them this afternoon. Will they be delivered to my house on Saturday, or do I need to make sure we pick them up?"

"They'll be delivered. It's just that everything needs to be confirmed and deposits dropped off." She started to pull her checkbook out of her bag. "I'll leave the amounts blank, and you can just fill them in."

I stared at her checkbook, my mouth open in surprise. Did she really think we were letting her pay for her wedding shower? "No," I said, pulling the pen out of her hand. "I've got this shindig covered."

"Jade," she said with a frown. "I can't ask you to pay for this elaborate party just because I've had this picture in my head for years. Don't worry, I've budgeted—"

"Forget it." I crossed my arms over my chest and shook my head. "You didn't ask me to pay for it. I offered. If it means that much to you, you can take care of my baby shower." I grinned at her. "I'm pulling rank. As your best friend, it's my prerogative to give you this gift, and there's nothing you can say to change my mind."

When Kat turned to Pyper for support, Pyper raised her

hands. "Don't look at me. I'm on Jade's side. In fact, we'll split the cost. You shouldn't have to pay for the shower we want to throw you. You've already planned it; that's quite enough." She winked at Kat and stabbed another piece of sashimi.

Kat sighed in defeat. "Fine. But if anything is too extravagant, don't hesitate to let me know. I'll pay for it. Got it?"

"Got it," I said, tracing an X over my heart. "Since we missed lunch, want to come over for dinner? Bring Lucien?"

"All right." A pleased smile transformed her previously gloomy expression, and her hazel eyes danced with excitement as she clapped her hands. "Oh gosh. I'm so excited. Saturday is going to be so much fun. I can't wait!"

"Me neither," I said with forced enthusiasm. It wasn't that I wasn't looking forward to the party. I definitely was. It was that I suddenly had a lot on my plate, and hauling myself around New Orleans in the ninety-degree heat was a lot to deal with while being seven months pregnant.

"Yay!" Kat positively glowed as she threw some bills on the table and grabbed her bag. "I have an appointment at the shop. Some guy wants a custom piece for his wife for their anniversary. Gotta go. See you tonight."

"Later!" Pyper said, eyeing the rest of the rainbow roll.

I waved to Kat and then looked at the food in front of us. There was raw fish everywhere. "This isn't going to work for me."

"Here. Fried rice. Looks like chicken." Pyper passed me a bowl.

I took one bite and raised my hand, signaling to the

waitress. The rice was cold. "Can I get a fresh one of these and a tempura shrimp roll?"

"Sure." The waitress disappeared into the back of the restaurant while I looked at the list Kat had left us.

"Want to start working on these after lunch?" I asked Pyper.

"Sure. What's up first?"

"The bakery. Says we need to approve the designs and leave a deposit. What's the design supposed to be? Did she tell us?" I turned the list over, looking for a clue, but found nothing.

Pyper shook her head. "Nope. I think that's what this lunch was supposed to be about."

I quickly sent Kat a text. It wasn't long before my food arrived, but Kat still hadn't responded by the time we were done.

"LUCIEN, THANK GOODNESS," I said into the phone when he answered. Pyper and I were sitting in her car, parked in front of the bakery Kat had sent us to. But we hadn't gone in because we still didn't know what we were approving. "Listen, Kat has us running some errands for the bridal shower. Do you have any idea what she ordered at the bakery? Or what the theme is supposed to be?"

"Um, no. Should I?" He sounded vaguely distracted.

"Lucien, focus. We're already in trouble here after missing lunch. Kat's a little bit hurt, and if we get this wrong—"

"Oh, I know. The sixties. That's the theme. She said something about daisies and sunflowers and lots of pink, orange, and yellow."

"Sixties? Really?" It sounded cute, but Kat was usually a little more modern than that in her ideas.

"Yep. She said she wanted to have fun with it."

"All right then. Now that we have that out of the way, I have something for you. Can you research a breeder out in the bayou by the name of Elijah? He breeds familiars. I don't have a last name, but I do have an address and a phone number."

"Sure. Does this have something to do with that fire-breathing dog?" he asked.

"Yes and no. He just seems to know quite a bit about the council, and I want to know who exactly we're dealing with. I think he might be an ally, but we just can't be too careful."

"I'm on it."

I rattled off the information and said, "By the way, you and Kat are coming to dinner tonight. I hope you didn't have plans."

"Nope. Whatever Kat wants these next few weeks, Kat gets," he said with a chuckle.

"Is she still being a bridezilla?" I asked with a grimace.

"No. Not at all. It's more like she's anxious. I'm not sure if it's because the day is finally almost here and she's experiencing a version of cold feet or if all the planning is getting to her. She's been focused on this wedding and little else for months. Whatever it is, we've made it this far. I'm sure we can handle the next two weeks."

"Damn," I said softly. "I'm sorry, Lucien. I had no idea.

She seems perfectly normal every time I see her. Busy and a little overloaded, but…" I paused, thinking back over the past month and the time I'd spent with Kat. It hadn't been a lot if I was honest with myself. Ever since she and Lucien had gotten engaged, she'd dragged Pyper and me all over the city to every bridal shop, bakery, and party store she could find. While Pyper had been decisive in her choices, Kat hadn't, and the strain of her indecision had worn me down. I'd begged off most things lately, using my pregnancy as an excuse. Now I was starting to wonder if my friend felt completely abandoned. "You know what? It's been a few weeks since Kat and I have had any time together. I'll talk to her tonight and find out what's up."

"You don't need to do that, Jade," he said, his tone wary. "She's my fiancée. If there's anything to work out, we'll figure it out."

"Of course you will," I said. "I just meant I'll check in with her and see how she's doing. Girl stuff. You know. See you tonight!" I ended the call, and Pyper and I went into the store where we approved the cutest VW cupcakes and daisy sugar cookies for the bridal shower.

CHAPTER 12

"We need to come up with some sort of plan for tomorrow," I said to Pyper as I washed the lettuce for the salad I was making. We'd worked our way through half of one of Kat's lists before exhaustion had taken over and Pyper had insisted on driving me home. She'd told me she wasn't going to be responsible if I fainted from overexertion. I'd rolled my eyes and told her she was being dramatic, but the truth was my back ached and so did my feet.

"Sit." She gently bumped me out of the way. "I'll deal with your salad fixings. You drink your decaf tea and relax."

I didn't hesitate. Kane would be grilling steaks and corn once he got home. My only job was the salad since I'd already picked up a chocolate torte for dessert at the bakery. "Okay. I'll make a list of places to go tomorrow to find Harper."

"Do you hear that?" Pyper asked, cocking her head to one side.

"What?" I glanced around the kitchen, trying to discern what she was talking about.

"It's coming from outside." She strode to the back door and flung it open.

A small brown dog darted in, her tongue lolling as she panted and headed straight for my feet.

"Flame? What the heck? Where did you come from?" I reached down and picked up the familiar. Her coat was hot like she'd spent hours in the sun. She blinked up at me, and I immediately checked her gums to see if she was dehydrated. Nope. Nice and pink. Good. Was it even possible for fire-breathing familiars to get dehydrated? I had no idea, but I wasn't taking any chances. "Pyper, can you get her some water?"

"Of course." She went to work on getting the pup a bowl of water while I scanned the backyard and checked the gate. No one was there and nothing was out of order.

I walked back in and closed the door. Without saying a word, I pulled out my phone and called Willa.

No answer. I left a message, letting her know I had Flame—err, Peanut—and told her to call at her earliest convenience to let me know she was all right.

"That's strange," Pyper said while we watched the dog lap up water.

I nodded. Why did Flame keep coming back to my house? Then I shrugged. It wasn't like I could ask Willa or Harper. "Maybe we should ask Elijah why she does that."

"Couldn't hurt."

I dug out his card and dialed the number. Then I frowned. It had been disconnected. I ended the call and tried again. Same result. Grimacing, I tossed his card into the trash and stared down at Flame. "Well, nothing to do but watch her until we find Harper I guess."

"Think you can keep her from burning your house down?"

"I'm gonna have to," I said and sat back down at the table. "I can't put her outside, and apparently no matter what, she's going to keep coming back. Might as well get used to her for a while."

Pyper leaned down and patted the familiar on the head. "At least she's cute."

"That's something I guess." I drummed my fingernails on the table and said, "Now, what were we talking about?"

"Our plan of action tomorrow," she said. "Harper's apartment seems like the obvious place to start."

"Right. The council too. If we can find Crescent La Croix, she might have some very valuable council information."

"She's the one who helped you expose Delphinia a few months ago at your hearing, right?"

I nodded. Delphinia had been trying to cover up her role in unleashing the dragon that had possessed Conor Wells. While I'd been locked up, Crescent had filled in the blanks with knowledge that had directly led to my release. "If the council is hiding anything, I bet she knows what it is."

"All right." Pyper had moved on to slicing red bell

peppers. "What about a finding spell? You could call in the coven and see if you can find Harper that way."

"Got it." I'd already scratched the suggestion down in my notes. Finding spells were taking it out of me lately. In some things I was strong, like controlling the weather. In others, like finding spells, it was like short-circuiting my power even with the coven there to back me up. "If all that fails… we could try summoning Harper's ancestor. She might be able to tap into the ancient magic to at least get a location on her."

"You mean summon a ghost," Pyper said.

"Yeah, well, I do know a talented medium."

"How would we do that?" Pyper asked, grabbing mushrooms from the fridge.

"I have a few ideas," I said. "But I bet Bea could tell us."

"Call her," Pyper said. "Our leads are really pathetic right now."

They were. We had hardly anything to go on, and it frustrated me. There was a young woman out there, probably scared to death, and here Pyper and I had been running party-planning errands. I picked up the phone and dialed Bea's number. No answer. I left a message. "So we have go to Harper's apartment, talk to Crescent at the council, and try a finding spell. Plus we're waiting for Bea to call back about summoning Harper's ancestor. What am I missing? We already talked to her cousins."

"Didn't Cami say Harper has a boyfriend? Music major?" Pyper said.

"Right. Violin first chair." I jotted that down on my list

and leaned down to pick up Flame, who was pawing at my leg. I snuggled the dog and said, "Good. Tomorrow we can get to work."

"And stop by the florist and the party store," Pyper added with a chuckle.

"WHO'S READY FOR DESSERT?" I asked, holding out my hand, silently asking Kane to help me off the couch. Kane, Lucien, Kat, and I had settled in the living room in the front of the house after dinner. Despite my invitation, Pyper hadn't stayed, instead insisting she needed to get home. Julius and Bo were on dinner duty, and she wasn't going to miss it for the world.

"Oh, I'll get it." Kat bounced out of her chair and started heading back to the kitchen.

"Wait for me." I smiled at my husband after he got me on my feet. Flame was right at my side like she had been all night, the perfectly behaved puppy. "Chocolate torte?"

"You know I would've gotten it, Jade," he whispered in my ear.

"I know." I kissed him on the cheek. "But I'm still able-bodied." I turned to Lucien. "Torte?"

His nose was stuck in a book and he didn't respond.

I chuckled softly. Lucien was sitting across the room, his blond hair sticking up in odd angles from running his fingers through it while studying a book on dragon lore. I cleared my throat. "Hey, Lucien."

His head jerked up. "Huh?"

"Wanna break for dessert? Chocolate torte?" I asked.

"Oh, sure." He started to close the book and rise from the chair.

"Stay there," I said. "We'll bring it out here. Coffee?"

"Yes, please." He immediately disappeared behind the book again, just as I knew he would. Lucien was very good at research.

By the time Flame and I caught up with Kat, she already had the coffee started and had plated two pieces of torte. "Hey. You're quick."

She smiled at me, and not for the first time that night, I noticed her tired eyes and the fatigue in her tense shoulders. "I guess I'm desperate for a little chocolate."

"Stressed?" I plated the second two pieces of torte.

She leaned against the counter and crossed her arms over her chest. She was wearing a red-and-white cupcake dress that made her look adorable and me feel like a smallish blimp. "I think it's just the countdown to the wedding. It's a lot, you know?"

I placed a hand on my belly and nodded my agreement. "We both have a lot of changes coming."

Her expression softened as she stared at me, and then her eyes got glassy as she said, "I can't wait to meet that sweet little girl."

Kat's emotion overwhelmed me. She was one big ball of love and excitement mixed with a trace of fear.

I gently took her hand in mine and said, "It's going to be great, you know."

"Of course it is. You always were meant to be a mother,

even when you were convinced it wasn't a good idea." Her words were so sincere I had to blink back tears.

"Thank you, Kat. That means the world to me. But I meant the wedding. Your life with Lucien. You two are perfect for each other. All the buildup, all the stress, none of it's going to matter when you're standing at that altar, staring at the man you love while he looks at you like you're the reason he breathes."

Silent tears rolled down her cheeks, and she pressed a hand over her heart. "How..." She sniffed. "How did you know that's what I needed to hear?"

"You're my oldest and best friend, Kat. I might be a little self-involved right now, but I'm still paying attention. I'm sorry if I've made you feel unimportant, letting you do the shower planning and missing lunch. I didn't mean to."

She shook her head, wiping at her tears. "I didn't feel unimportant."

I raised a skeptical eyebrow.

"Okay, maybe just a little forgotten. You have the baby, and Pyper's wedding is coming up too. And I know I've been driving you both a little bit crazy with my inability to make decisions. I just... I don't know. I think I would've liked to have my mom here for the planning."

I gave her a curious look. "She didn't want to come down?"

Kat pressed her lips into a thin line. "She won't fly. She's not even coming for the wedding."

"What about driving? I know Idaho is a long way, but—"

"Mom's anxiety," Kat said, shaking her head. "She doesn't do well in the car either."

"Oh, honey. Why didn't you say anything?" I opened my arms wide for a hug, and she flung her arms around me.

"It wasn't... I don't know. I guess I hoped she'd change her mind," she said, her voice halting with tears.

All this time she'd been stressed that her mom wasn't coming for the wedding and she'd kept it in. "What about your dad?"

"He... won't... leave her."

My heart broke for Kat. And I thought my parents had issues. "Okay. Fine. How about this? Kane will give you away, and Bea can fill in as mother of the bride."

Kat pulled away. "Do you think Bea would mind?"

"I think she'll be honored. And about Kane, you don't even need to think twice. Or if he isn't acceptable, I'll do it myself." I grinned. "But you might have to slow your pace. I'm not moving as fast as I used to."

She chuckled. "As much as I'd love for you to be my escort, I think I'll stick with Kane. He looks better in a tux."

I snorted and hugged her again. Then I grew serious. "I know it hurts about your parents, Kat," I whispered. "But your chosen family loves you, and anything you need, we're here."

She choked back another sob and just nodded, clutching me tighter. When she got herself back under control, she pulled away. "Thanks, Jade. I needed that."

I grabbed her hand and squeezed again. "It's going to be okay. And when it's all done and you've had a proper honeymoon, maybe you and Lucien can think about going to visit them in Idaho for a bit. I'd be willing to bet your mom is feeling just as bad about not being here as you are."

"You're probably right. It's not her fault she has a phobia of flying."

But phobias could be overcome. I made a mental note to call my own mother. There was a good chance she might be able to help. "Come on," I said. "The coffee's done. Time to bliss out on chocolate."

CHAPTER 13

I turned over on my side and reached for my phone. Kane was sound asleep on his side of the bed, and Flame was curled up in a small dog bed I'd gotten from a neighborhood pet store, while I'd been lying awake for hours. Or at least it felt like hours. The chocolate torte had been a mistake. Not only was the chocolate keeping me wide awake, it had also given me heartburn.

The time on my phone read 4:42 a.m. I let out a sigh and flipped the cover off, giving up. My back ached, and the baby was restless. It was clear that sleep wasn't going to happen. I started to get out of bed but stopped when Kane's large hand landed on my thigh.

"Where are you going?" he asked, his voice groggy with sleep.

"To the couch," I said quietly. "I don't want to keep you awake with my restlessness."

"You weren't." His voice was clearer, and he sat up, scooting closer to me. "What's the problem? Back? Shoulders? Legs?"

I let out a small laugh. "All of the above. Everything aches."

"I can help." He moved to sit behind me and propped himself against the headboard as he started to knead my shoulders.

"Kane," I said. "You don't have— Oh. That's really good."

"Just relax, shortcake. I've got you," he whispered into my ear.

I leaned back against him, finally relaxing as his hands roamed over me, easing the tension from my aching muscles. My eyes grew heavy, and small moans of pleasure escaped my parted lips. Before I knew it, his hands were no longer massaging; instead, he was caressing me... everywhere. My hips, my sides, my breasts.

Kane's warm lips trailed up my neck, and in the faintest whisper, he said, "You're so lovely. Lush. Glorious. And I want you more than ever."

"Okay," I breathed and let myself get lost in everything his hands were promising.

"KNOCK, KNOCK!" a bright, cheerful voice called, waking me from my bliss. "Rise and shine, lazybones. We have a dragon to find."

I opened one eye, spotted Pyper and her smug smile, and then groaned. "It's too early. Go away."

"It's past nine. Don't make me drag you out of there." She opened the shade on the window and sunlight poured in. "Kane made you breakfast."

That got my attention. I pushed myself up into a sitting position "French toast? Omelet? Pancakes?"

"You'll just have to get up to find out." She disappeared into the bathroom, and a second later the pipes groaned as water rushed through them into the shower. When she reappeared, she asked, "Want me to pick your clothes out too?"

I grinned at her as I hefted myself out of the bed. "Sure. Just make sure it's not black." Today she was wearing beige linen capris and a formfitting white tank top that showed off her figure along with ballet flats. "You look nice."

"Thanks. I'm hoping to avoid heatstroke." She pointed to the bathroom. "Get moving."

Twenty minutes later, I emerged from my bedroom, showered and wearing another sundress. This one was white with gorgeous red hibiscus flowers on it.

"French toast!" I exclaimed, making a beeline for the table. "Omigod. My husband is amazing."

Pyper laughed and put a mug in front of me. "Decaf chai."

I made goo-goo eyes at her. "If I wasn't already married, I'd steal you from Julius."

"I know." She sat down opposite me with her own plate of french toast.

Flame trotted over from where she'd been standing near the dog dish and sat at my feet. I reached down and patted her on the head. "Did you get breakfast and go out?"

"Kane said he took care of her," Pyper said.

"Perfect." I dug into my french toast, surprised it was warm. Pyper must've heated it up for me while I was in the shower. I was halfway through my breakfast before I realized Pyper wasn't eating. I glanced up at her. "What is it?"

Her brows were pinched together, and she was frowning. "I'm not sure. I had a strange dream last night. I think…" She paused and shook her head. "No, I *know* that a ghost visited me in my dreams. And I think it was a warning about Harper."

I put my fork down. "Who was it? What did they say?"

She let out a frustrated sigh. "I'm not sure who she was. She was… unfocused. Frantic maybe. She just kept saying, 'He can't be trusted.' But I have no idea who *he* is. And even though she didn't tell me her name, I have a really strong feeling she's Harper's ancestor. It was something about the eyes."

"Whoa," I said, my entire body on alert. The council had said that Pyper's gift was needed. How did they know a ghost would visit her? "Okay. That's strange. What do you think of the warning? Who could he be?"

"I've been going over it in my head, and the only man in her life that we know about is her boyfriend. Right? The violinist?"

"Yes. What about Mr. Elijah? Or Vic at the store she worked at?" I frowned and shook my head. "Other than the familiar, Mr. Elijah didn't seem to be involved in her life."

"And Vic just seemed more annoyed at the

inconvenience of Harper leaving than anything else," she added.

"Right. So the boyfriend it is then. Should we go see him first?" I asked as I forked another piece of french toast.

"Seems like the logical place to start." She sipped from her coffee mug, and her features smoothed out as if she was relieved just to have shared the troubling visit with me. Then she glanced at Flame. "What's your plan for her today? Take her with us, or..."

"Kane got a crate at the pet store yesterday evening. Let's put her there while we're out."

IT DIDN'T TAKE LONG to find the music department at Tulane. The orchestra was highly regarded and played all over the city. The students who excelled were celebrated, and Liam Colman was no exception. The minute I'd asked about the first violinist chair, one of the faculty went on and on about how brilliant he was and then pointed us to the Dixon Concert Hall.

"He's working on his showcase. And I must say it's brilliant," the woman said with a heartfelt sigh. Her gray hair hung down her back all the way past her butt. She looked every bit the sixties hippie with her long cotton skirt, a shapeless white blouse, and leather flip-flops. There was even a silver ring on her second toe. The only thing missing was a crown of daisies on her head. "Are you here to recruit him for a performance?"

I started to shake my head, but Pyper said, "Yes. We have

a wedding coming up in a few months, and we're looking for a few classically trained musicians for the reception."

"Oh, isn't that lovely." She grinned at my belly. "Isn't it sweet you're starting a family? I guess that means it's time to tie the knot, huh?" The woman winked at me. "Even the best of us fall for conventions every once in a while, right?"

Pyper chuckled and took my hand in hers, caressing it with her thumb. "Isn't it lovely that it's legal now?"

The woman placed a hand over her heart and sighed with so much emotion I thought she might cry. "Yes. Yes, it is. Aren't you two just lovely? I'm so happy for you." She glanced at the wall clock behind us. "Oh, look at that. I have to run. Congratulations and good luck!" She wiggled her fingers and took off down the hall.

I yanked my hand out of Pyper's and shook my head at her. "You're bad, you know that?"

She threw her head back and laughed. "It's not my fault she made assumptions. I just thought it was easier to let her think whatever she wanted to."

Rolling my eyes, I turned around and made my way out of the building. As she followed, her trepidation and unease suddenly tickled my skin. I paused and glanced around, alarmed. "What is it?"

"Huh?" She scanned the area. "Do you feel something?"

"Yeah, but it's coming from you. What has you worried?"

"Oh." She started to chuckle again, only this time it was tinged with nervousness. "I was worried you took offense to my pretending we were engaged."

I turned and stared at her, my mouth open in surprise. Then I frowned. "Why?"

"I don't know." She shrugged. "You just seemed… a little uncomfortable I guess."

"Pyper, please." I started walking again, eager to get out of the sun. "The only reason I'd be uncomfortable is because you're like a sister to me. I'm not offended. Actually, it was pretty funny. I was just confused about why you didn't tell her the truth."

"Oh, because I thought she'd tell us not to bother him. The showcase is a *huge* deal." We neared the music hall, and Pyper reached for the door, pulling it open for me. "That's where students are recruited for placement in orchestras and other productions after graduation. I didn't want her to tell us we couldn't interrupt him."

"Right." That made sense. "Quick thinking."

"Thanks."

The moment we walked into the building, the haunting sound of a violin consumed me. And without any conscious thought, I gravitated to it as if the music was calling to my very soul. The sound filled me up, sending my blood humming, and I just felt *alive.*

My footsteps were soft while all my aches and pains vanished. All that mattered was the music.

I floated into the concert hall and spotted a tall, handsome young man in the middle of the stage, a violin on his shoulder as he ran the bow over the strings with power and determination written all over his features. But that wasn't all. There were two violins on either side of him, floating in the air, their bows independently flying over the strings, helping to create a symphony of violin magic.

"He's incredible," Pyper said.

I didn't answer her as I moved forward, needing to be closer.

"Jade?"

I heard Pyper behind me, but I didn't care. I *needed* to be one with the music. The gravitational pull had completely consumed me, and it wasn't until I was in the front row that I slowly took a seat, staring up at the young man and his collection of violins in complete awe.

Liam Colman's spell had so thoroughly compelled me that by the time the last notes of his performance reverberated through the hall, I was ready to beg him for more. I stood on shaky legs, my entire body trembling, and whistled my approval, clapping my hands as tears ran down my face.

"Snap out of it, Jade!" Pyper shook my arm.

"Huh?" I glanced over and found her giving me a strange look.

"We need to move. He's getting away."

I blinked and glanced back at the stage. The young man was standing there, smiling at me, while the floating violins danced around him. "No, he isn't. He's—" The violins suddenly vanished, and Liam started to fade into the ether. "Dammit! It was an illusion."

"That's what I was trying to tell you." She tugged my arm. "Come on. He ran out the back."

I glanced down at my belly and shook my head. "You go. See if you can track him. I'm going to search the hall in case he left anything behind."

"Got it." She jumped up onto the stage and took off at a dead run.

I wondered briefly how she'd known it was an illusion when I hadn't been able to tell, but I didn't dwell on it. Pyper might not be magical, but she had other gifts that served her well, like her ability to see and speak to ghosts. Maybe one of them had clued her in.

After taking a deep breath to center myself, I sent out my magic, searching for any traces of emotional energy. If Liam was in the building still, I might be able to find him. A faint trace of guilt brushed over my skin. I retreated back through the theater, following the prickling feeling. It intensified when I found myself in the lobby, but as I moved toward the front doors, it started to fade. I turned left and headed up the stairs, once again on track.

The emotional signature intensified, and soon I found myself in the balcony overlooking the theater. Someone was there, I just couldn't see anyone.

"Hello?" I called. My voice echoed through the space. "Who's here?"

Nothing.

"I'm just looking for some information. I'm not here to get anyone in trouble."

Still nothing. But then the faint sound of soft footsteps near the stairs on the other side of the balcony caught my attention. On instinct, I threw out a bolt of magic and cried, "*Ipsum revelare!*"

The stream of light crackled in the air, hit its mark, and illuminated a medium-build, dark-skinned young man wearing a purple ball cap. His back was to me as he ran down the stairs, and as soon as my magic faded, so did his image.

"Concealing spell," I said to myself. In my current condition, I wasn't going to be chasing anyone. However, it was clear our trip to see Liam Colman was a step in the right direction. He and his cohort were definitely up to something. Finding Liam had just become priority number one.

I slowly made my way back out to the front of the building and leaned against the brick wall while texting Pyper to let her know where I was waiting for her.

Her text arrived instantly. *Be right there.*

A minute later, she reappeared, her face damp with sweat.

"Any luck?" I asked.

Pyper shook her head. "No. Nothing. I thought I spotted him getting into a white Jeep Wrangler, but when I got closer, it was actually a woman with short hair, same sort of build." Her expression turned frustrated. "I could've sworn that was him. It doesn't make sense."

"I think someone's been playing with illusion spells," I said, leading her away from the building and filling her in on what I'd experienced. "I don't know why, but it appears Liam Colman doesn't want to talk to us. And he probably has an accomplice or two."

"Are you saying I was fooled by an illusion spell? That Liam wasn't Liam at all?"

I shrugged. "Maybe. Or it's possible that was him and he cast an illusion to get you off his trail. I don't know, but I am sure it's more important than ever to track him down."

Pyper pulled out her phone and tapped the screen. "Julius? Yeah, I need you to run a search on someone. Get us a home address and work address if applicable. Liam Colman, Tulane University student. Music major. Thanks." She tapped another button, ending the call. "He'll text us the information as soon as possible."

"It's good having connections," I said. "Let's get to Harper's apartment. See if we can find anything there."

CHAPTER 14

The one-bedroom apartment was only a few blocks away, but due to the heat, we took Pyper's car. Willa finally called me back, letting me know she had no idea how Flame escaped but was glad she was safe. And after I told her we were headed to Harper's apartment, she said she'd meet us there.

When we pulled up in front of the building, I groaned. Fitch and Myers, Creepy Cop and Good Cop from the council, were outside, interviewing people. "Looks like the council isn't taking any chances."

Pyper gritted her teeth. "Assholes."

I laughed and hauled myself out of the car.

"Ladies," Creepy Cop Fitch said, his tone somehow making the word sound like a come-on. "Miss me?"

I walked right past him toward the fourplex. Pyper flipped him the finger.

Good Cop Myers laughed.

We ignored him too and walked right into the building as if we owned it. Harper's apartment was on the top floor, facing the busy street. Light streamed through the window, illuminating dust motes and the piles of personal items upended all over the room.

"Son of a... Did those council clowns do this?" Pyper asked.

"You can't be in here," Fitch said from behind us. I'd known he was there, had already felt his gleeful energy as he followed us up the stairs, but I'd chosen to ignore him. Now he'd given me no choice.

"Go away, jackass," I said, annoyed and tired. "If you haven't heard, we've been tasked by the council with finding Harper. Searching her apartment is standard procedure."

"We've got that covered," Fitch insisted, his hand slipping into his pocket. The fabric was already bulging, and it had nothing to do with his man-package. "You'll be notified if there's anything of interest."

"What's that in your pocket?" I asked.

Self-satisfaction streamed off him in waves of putrid body odor that smelled like rotten oranges, and I decided right then and there that Fitch's soul was rotten to the core. Should he be a suspect? I made a mental note to put him on the list. I'd engaged with my fair share of council witches over the years. Some were self-serving, some were plain evil, and some were just decent witches trying to do their jobs. But this guy? He was vindictive and clearly got off on power. He seemed the type who would snatch women and hide them away in a bayou shack in order to build a dragon army.

He leered at me, pumped his eyebrows, and sidled up next to me, rubbing his thigh on my hip. "Want to find out?"

"If you don't stop touching me—"

"If you don't stop touching me," he echoed in a mocking voice. "What are you gonna do about it, white witch? Gonna go toe-to-toe with the big bad wolf? And while you're knocked up no less?" He threw his head back and laughed. "You're playing with fire, little girl."

"Keep talking and you'll find out real quick what I'm capable of, *Fitch*," I said with a snarl, ready to crush his balls with my bare hands.

His face turned to stone as he stared me down with his icy gaze. "You're a pawn, Jade Calhoun. Don't think the council gives two shits about you. If someone needs to take the fall for this, it'll be you. Mark my words. Now play ball or get the hell out of the way."

I had no doubt he was speaking the truth. If dragons came to power in New Orleans, the council would have to blame it on someone. It suddenly made sense why they'd picked Pyper and me up and forced us to work for them. We'd be the fall guys. But I wasn't going to let that happen. I took two steps back, putting distance between us, and met his contemptuous glare with one of my own. "And what exactly is it I'm expected to do in order to play ball?"

"Isn't it obvious?" he asked, shaking his head in disbelief. "You work with the council, not against us. And that means sharing information."

"You first." I crossed my arms over my chest and briefly cut my gaze to the bulge in his pocket.

His lips curved into that sleazy smile again. "I'll show you the goods later. Right now, you and your freak sidekick need to vacate the property. You don't have authorization to be here."

"Yes, she does," Willa said, storming in, her eyes blazing with contempt. She stopped beside me and faced Fitch. "I'm Harper's cousin and next of kin. You have to get permission from me to search her place." She pointed at Fitch. "You're the one who's trespassing. I suggest you leave before the NOPD gets here."

"They don't have jurisdiction over the council," Fitch said, not moving.

"Do you have a warrant?" I asked him. "Or permission from Harper to enter her residence?" I knew the answer to both was no. The council didn't bother with warrants. They conducted business in their own way. The NOPD would back them up, but not until it went up the chain. If a rank-and-file officer showed up, Fitch and Myers would be asked to leave.

"We're done here anyway," Myers said, suddenly appearing in the room. "Come on, Fitch. We need to get back to the council grounds anyway."

"Not until you show me what's in that pocket," I said. "What are you taking, Fitch?"

"None of your damned business." He turned and started to make his way out into the hall.

What a complete jackass. There was no way I was letting him get away with walking out of there with whatever was in his pocket. Without an ounce of guilt, I called my magic up. But instead of throwing a bolt of magic at him, I imagined the thread in his pocket unraveling and whatever he'd taken falling out onto the carpet in the hallway.

"You're just going to let him leave?" Willa asked incredulously.

I nodded and whispered, "Wait for it."

We both moved to the open door and watched as Myers and Fitch strode to the stairwell. Just as they took their first steps, a gorgeous blue geode tumbled silently to the floor. Fitch never even looked back.

I grinned at her, calmly walked over and grabbed the geode, and made my way back into the room, hoping Fitch wouldn't notice it was gone until he and Myers were back at council headquarters.

When I heard the front door slam, I turned to Willa. "Any idea what this is and why they wanted it?"

She frowned and started to shake her head, but as she took it in her hand, her mouth dropped open and she let out a small gasp. "Jade," she whispered. "It's calling to me."

"What?" I took it back from her, trying to understand what she was experiencing. But all I felt was a cool piece of rock that didn't even carry any energy. Or at least no human energy. I put it back into her hand, wrapped her fingers around it, and raised my hand, stopping her when she tried to talk. "Give me a minute. I want to try something."

She stilled, and I called my magic to the surface, pushing it toward her, reading her.

Her energy overwhelmed me, soaking into me bone

deep. A familiar wave of awe and urgency consumed me, and it didn't take me long to figure out Willa was experiencing the same phenomenon that I had back at the music hall. Like she was compelled to seek someone or something out.

I let go of her hands and asked, "Where is it you want to be right at this moment?"

"What?" She blinked at me as if confused, but I could still feel her energy, and her reaction to me was forced, as if she instinctively knew she should keep her thoughts to herself.

"Willa, this is important. I know you feel compelled to go somewhere or find someone. It's the magic in the geode. Can you tell me where?"

She dropped the geode and clutched her hands together, her entire body going rigid. "I... It's not the geode." Shaking her head, she wiped a tear from her cheek. "I didn't mean to fall for him. It was... I'd never do something like that to Harper."

"*Liam Colman*? Harper's boyfriend?" I asked, my heart racing. "You want to be with him?"

"I love my boyfriend!" she cried. "I didn't ask for this. What is happening right now?" She buried her face in her hands, and her shoulders shook with silent sobs.

Out of the corner of my eye, I saw Pyper pick up the geode and shove it into her shoulder bag. Then she signaled she'd be outside. I nodded to her and turned my attention back to the young woman in front of me.

"Willa," I said gently. "There's magic infused in that rock. Have you seen it before? Touched it before?"

"Yes. About a month ago when Liam gave it to Harper.

She has a thing for these." Willa waved a hand at the collection on the shelf to her right.

I eyed them and picked up an amethyst one and then a pink one. Both seemed harmless enough. "Have you considered that it's not you? That you've been spelled?"

She shook her head. "It's not that."

"Are you sure?" I reached out and gently took one of her hands and put the pink geode in her palm. The awe and urgency were gone, and all I felt was sadness and disappointment. I repeated the process with the amethyst one. Nothing changed.

"I just... I can't stop thinking about him. I either can't wait to see him again or I'm depressed about the entire thing. I don't want to want Liam. I want to want Lucas."

"Is Lucas your boyfriend?" I asked.

"Yes." She lifted her tear-streaked face. "He's wonderful. Kind, smart, funny. And he loves me. Liam..." She scowled. "He's moody, self-absorbed, and arrogant because of his talent. He has his moments when he's kind and sensitive with Harper, but they're few and far between. I don't know why I can't get him out of my head."

I knew. No matter what she believed, I was certain that Liam was using his magic to compel people, to put a spell on them to bend them to his will. His music had transfixed even me, but it was more than just his playing. There'd been magic in the air in that hall, and I was certain the music had been the vehicle to deliver it. I wasn't sure why or how, but the magic from Liam's violin matched the magic in the blue geode. The star violinist was smack in the middle of this, and I needed to figure out why.

"How long has this been going on?" I asked her.

"Two, three weeks, I guess." She sank down onto the messy bed that had piles of ransacked clothes on it. "One day the three of us were hanging out, and Liam started to play his violin. I was transfixed, lost in his music. It was hauntingly gorgeous. Ever since then..." She let out a sigh and clutched at her heart. "He touched me, you know? And now I can't get him out of my head."

I frowned. The music. His magic was in his music.

"Willa, listen to me," I said.

She lifted her gaze to mine.

"I want you to stay away from Liam for now. No matter what, just keep your distance, okay? I think you've been spelled."

Willa opened her mouth to no doubt contradict me, but I shook my head, stopping her.

"Even if you're not, you obviously don't want to hurt your cousin. Or your boyfriend, who you told me you love, right?"

"Right." Her voice was small, full of guilt and confusion.

"Then do us both a favor and just keep your distance. It's better for all of you. And it will give me time to figure out what's going on." I stood and held out my hand to her. "Now, do you want to help me look through this stuff? I'm trying to find clues as to where Harper could be."

At the mention of her cousin's name, resolve seemed to settle in her dark gaze and she nodded. "Yes. I'll stay away from Liam. You're right. It's better for everyone." She glanced around the room. "Now, what are we looking for?"

"Anything that looks like a random address, a journal, or anything unusual or tinged with magic," I said.

"Okay. I'm on it." Willa stepped into the closet and reached for the shoeboxes on the top shelf.

When the boxes turned out to be filled with actual shoes, I turned to the desk and got to work.

CHAPTER 15

"That was… interesting," Pyper said. She was back behind the wheel, and we were headed to the florist to take care of Kat's deposit. "Did you find anything that might help locate Harper?"

I shook my head. "Nothing. I'm betting if there was anything, Creepy Cop and Good Cop already got it. But we do have the geode they wanted, so that's something." I glanced at the rock sitting in the cup holder in the console between us. "At this point, I think we need to keep focusing on Liam. I think he's behind the disappearance of the women."

"Any proof?"

"No. Not really. But his magic is unsettling, and the fact that it's in the geode that Creepy Cop was trying to take makes me suspicious. Besides, why did Liam run this morning when all we wanted to do was talk to him? There's something there. As soon as Julius gets us his information, we'll check out his place and talk to any coworkers."

"Okay. Sounds like a plan." She pulled the car to a stop in front of the Bloomin' Idiot. "Kat did get her flowers here, right?"

I glanced at the list Kat had given me. "Yep."

"Good. If she didn't use Miss Maybelle, we were going to have words." Pyper's tone was teasing, but I suspected there was some truth behind them. We'd found the Bloomin' Idiot a few months ago while shopping for wedding florals for both Pyper's and Kat's big days, and Miss Maybelle had turned out to be incredible. Kane had even started going by periodically to buy me flowers just to surprise me.

We strolled in, and the sweet scent of jasmine washed over me. I took a deep breath, letting the florals cleanse the events of the day away.

"Jade, Pyper." Miss Maybelle hobbled out from behind the counter. Her white mane of hair was pulled back into a long, low ponytail, and her eyes were bright with happiness as she took my hand. "Look at the mama-to-be. How are you feeling? Ready to meet that sweet little girl?"

"I'm more than ready," I said with a smile and then chuckled. "If this is what it feels like to be seven months pregnant, I can't imagine what nine months will be like."

She laughed softly and patted my hand. "You'll get through it."

"I hope so." I dug around in my bag and pulled out my wallet. "We're actually here to pay the deposit for Kat's flowers for this weekend and to arrange the delivery."

"Ah, yes." She reached for her order book and flipped it

open. "The wedding shower for Katrina. Crowns and centerpieces made of sunflowers and daisies. This Saturday, deliver by eleven a.m. Yes?"

"Sounds about right," I said with a chuckle. Sunflowers and daisies to go with Kat's sixties theme.

She rattled off an amount and my address since we were hosting the event. After we paid, she lifted her hand close to my belly and asked, "May I?"

"Sure." I didn't usually let people touch my stomach, but Miss Maybelle was an exception. She'd been the one to first tell me we were having a girl.

Miss Maybelle pressed her aged hand against my belly and closed her eyes. She made a small concerned noise as her lips curved down.

"What is it?" I asked, suddenly worried. "What did you see?"

She pulled her hand away and met my gaze. Miss Maybelle's voice was low and full of urgency. "I see danger for you and your daughter, Jade. It's coming, and it's coming soon. Take precautions, because something evil is lurking, waiting to strike."

Fear coiled down my spine, and for the first time since I'd found out I was a witch, I wanted to run back to my house, lock myself in, and let the world take care of itself. Nothing was more important than my daughter.

"Jade," Miss Maybelle said, placing both hands on my shoulders. "It's a vision, not reality. You can change the outcome—you know that, right?"

"She does," Pyper said, her voice a little shaky.

I glanced over at my friend. She'd gone completely white

and she looked stricken, as if evil had already done its worst.

"Pyper, stop looking at me like that." My tone was strong and full of bravado I didn't really feel. But I'd be damned if I let myself succumb to fear. "I'm fine and so is the baby. And no one, I mean *no one*, is going to hurt my baby."

"There you go, child," Miss Maybelle said. "That's the kind of fire that will keep both of you safe."

"PYPER, COME ON," I said to my friend, trying to keep the exasperation from my voice.

After our visit with Miss Maybelle, Pyper had insisted on going back to my house for lunch and to discuss Miss Maybelle's warning. We were currently standing in the kitchen, staring each other down. Flame was curled around my feet, clearly happy to be out of the crate.

"You can't wrap me in a bubble. I have work to do. Women to save."

"*You* don't have to." She placed her hands on her hips and gave me a stern look. "I can. Julius can. So can Kane or Lucien or Bea. Hell, I can even call Lailah or Rosalee. *You* don't have to be at the center of this."

As much as I hated to admit it, she was right. I wasn't essential to this fight. Sure, I felt a sense of responsibility and the council had ordered me to find Harper, but that didn't mean I had to be stupid about it. There was nothing wrong with leaning on my friends when I needed to.

I let out a heavy sigh. "Do you have any idea how hard it is to sit on the sidelines and wait for news?"

"Yes. I do." Her expression softened. "Think about all the times I've been the one waiting for you and Kane, not knowing what was going on or if you two were going to make it back safely to us."

That had happened more often than I could count. I nodded and slumped into a kitchen chair. "What am I going to do with myself?"

"Help Kat finish her wedding shower charms?" She poured a couple of glasses of lemonade and sat down next to me. "Bake chocolate chip cream cheese cupcakes?"

My mouth watered. "Now that's truly evil. You know I'm trying to eat healthy for the baby."

"Please. You scarfed down french toast for breakfast. A cupcake isn't going to hurt."

"One won't. Twelve will." I got up and opened the fridge, scanning for food. Suddenly I was starving. I went to work on lunch and was just about done making us a couple of sandwiches when Kane burst in.

"Jade!" he called from the living room.

"We're back here," I called back and added, "as usual."

His emotions were a storm of fear, frustration, and downright anger as he strode over to me, instantly wrapping his arms around me. "You okay?"

I pressed my palm to his chest and pushed him back just a touch so that I could look up into his gaze. "Is there a reason I shouldn't be?"

"Pyper sent a text. She said to come home. That you were in danger."

"Pyper!" I admonished, glaring at her. "Was that necessary?"

She rolled her eyes. "That is not what I texted. I just told him what Miss Maybelle said. And I wanted backup because I thought you'd fight me when I said you had to step back on this case."

Kane pulled away from me and took out his phone. "It says 'Meet us at your place. Miss Maybelle says danger is lurking for Jade and the baby.' You think I'm supposed to be calm about that?"

"Nothing has happened yet, Kane," I said patiently and reached down to pick up Flame, needing to comfort myself with her snuggles. "It was just a warning." Ever since Miss Maybelle predicted the gender of our baby, I'd come to realize she was a gifted seer. If she saw something, it was best to pay attention. "I'm not fighting Pyper. I'll stay out of the fray. But she's going to need backup if she's going to keep looking for Harper. Can you take some time off to help her?"

Kane moved in, wrapped one arm tightly around me, and held Flame and me to him as if he never wanted to let go. "I think I should stay and keep an eye on you."

"Oh no you don't." I shook my head. "What's going to happen to me if I'm just sitting in my house, minding my own business? Pyper needs help. Women are disappearing. They're the ones we should be worried about. Not me."

"I'm always going to worry about my family, Jade," he said, his expression so earnest it made my heart squeeze.

I placed my free hand on his cheek, loving him more than ever, if that was even possible. "How about this? I'll stay home and take care of our little girl while you go and watch Pyper's back. I'll even call Kat and see if she can come babysit me. Or I'll go to her and help her at her shop."

"I'd feel better if you went to Bea's shop," he said.

"Fine. I'll go visit Bea," I said. "Happy now?"

"No." He gently took Flame and then tightened his arms around me and pulled me in, hugging me close. "I'll be happy when the council takes their order and shoves it up their asses."

Pyper laughed. "Me too."

"Won't we all." I smiled up at my husband. "I love you. And our little peanut. Now let's have lunch before you and Pyper have to go check out Harper's boyfriend." I glanced over at Pyper. "Julius sent his information, right?"

Pyper nodded. "Yep. He managed to pull it up before he got sent out on another case."

"Good. While you guys are gone, I'll call Lucien and see if he's learned anything more about dragons."

"But if you learn anything, you'll pass it on to us, right?" Pyper asked.

"You won't rush out to save anyone, right?" Kane added.

I clenched my fist, trying not to let my irritation get the better of me. "I'm not foolish, you know."

They shared a look that didn't go unnoticed.

"Dammit, you two." I lost the battle. My frustration was on full display as I stalked over to the fridge and yanked out the lemonade pitcher. "You know I can't just do *nothing* if someone is in danger."

Kane, who had more patience than a saint, gently took the pitcher from my hands and said, "We know. That's why we're worried. Please, just promise you won't be the one running into the middle of a crisis." He pressed his hand to my belly and stared into my eyes, his chocolate ones silently pleading with me. "For the baby's sake."

"I promise." What else could I possibly say? It wasn't as if I didn't take Miss Maybelle's warning seriously. I absolutely did. But their inability to understand I wasn't going to be stupid was wearing on me. "You can stop your worrying now. Both of you. I'll stay in the house for the next two months, eating bonbons and watching *Witchin' Hills* reruns until I can recite every last line. Sound good?"

"Like you don't already know most of the lines to *Witchin' Hills*," Pyper said with a snort.

I ignored her, grabbed my sandwich, and let the other two fend for themselves.

CHAPTER 16

*B*oredom was stuffing over a hundred sachets with herbs and dried petals. I'd kept my word, and before Pyper and Kane left to investigate Liam Colman, they'd dropped Flame and me off at Bea's shop. I'd called Bea earlier to ask if it was a good time to come by, and she'd been overjoyed. The minute I got to her shop, she put me in charge of finishing the wedding favors for Kat and Lucien's big day.

Bea's contribution was a gentle spell designed to bring love, peace, and prosperity to Kat's guests. She described the spell as more of a suggestion. If Kat's guests were open to the spell, it would help pave the way for positive events. If they weren't, nothing would come of it.

My eyes started to water, and I desperately wished for a nap. Or a coffee. Neither was in my future, but a cupcake could be. I finished filling the last of the sachets and then put Flame's leash on and we made our way from the back room of Bea's shop into the main store area.

My mentor was behind the counter, smiling at a young woman who was purchasing a variety of prepackaged spells designed for the tourists of the city, not necessarily the magical community. I waved as I walked past and said, "Headed to the Grind. Want anything?"

"Iced latte, please. Thank you, dear," Bea said and turned her attention back to her customer.

"Got it." I strolled out of the pleasantly air-conditioned shop and was immediately hit with a wave of humidity so thick it made my limbs feel as if I were walking through water. Good goddess, New Orleans was oppressive in August. Still, I was willing to brave the heat. I needed something to keep my mind off what was happening with Kane and Pyper. Liam appeared to be a powerful witch, and if he was the one who was abducting the women, then he was very dangerous. Not that Kane didn't have impressive skills himself. He was a demon hunter after all. I just wasn't used to being left out of the fight.

The Grind was only a handful of blocks away, but by the time I got there, I was dragging. Flame, however, didn't seem any worse for wear. She bounced into the shop, happy as could be, still no fire-breathing in sight. Me, on the other hand—my lower back, shoulders, and feet were aching again. If I hadn't already offered to get Bea a latte, I'd have just gone home and to bed. Instead, I ordered a couple of cupcakes, a scone, a cookie, and a bottle of water along with Bea's iced latte from Bo, who refused to let me pay.

"Thank you," I said and stuffed a twenty into the tip jar.

"You know you don't have to do that," he said, nodding to the tip jar. "Pyper would kill me if she found out I let you or Kane pay for anything."

"I do know." I smiled at him. "But the service is so great —I'm just doing what I'd normally do."

"Here you go, Jade," Reagan said, handing me Bea's latte and my water. "Try to stay cool today, huh? I hear we're supposed to have record heat."

"Really?" I checked the weather app on my phone. The heat index was close to 110 degrees. Yikes! I'd been so uncomfortable for the past month that I hadn't even really noticed the change. I grimaced. "You're right. Good thing I'm headed back to Bea's. She has great air-conditioning."

I waved, and Flame and I left to navigate the steamy streets of the French Quarter back to Bea's shop. It was late afternoon, and Bourbon Street had that slight lingering stench of rotten garbage despite the smaller late-summer crowds. I held my breath and hurried down the street, trying to keep my nausea at bay.

Keeping my head down and my face out of the sun, I turned left to get off Bourbon and onto one of the quieter streets, Flame trotting just ahead of me. The stench faded almost immediately, and I started to relax my shoulders.

But then I stopped when I felt dread and unease crawl up my back. Flame growled and... was that smoke coming out of her nostrils? I inched closer to the building and turned to glance around. No one was there. Not behind me or on the other side of the street. Tourists were still milling around on Bourbon, and I saw some crossing Royal a block down, but the side street I was on was empty.

Only it wasn't. I could feel the ominous energy, and it was headed straight for me.

It's an illusion, I thought for the second time that day. It had to be. Magic sprang to my palms. Without thought, I let go of my goods. They floated in the air near me as I placed my palms out in front of me for protection, calling, "*Ipsum revelare!*"

My magic spilled out of my hands, hitting nothing but heavy, humid air. I spun around, throwing my magic in the other direction, and hit pay dirt.

A small redhead materialized, her face set in a smug smile. "Jade, exactly the woman I was looking for."

Flame yanked on her leash, growling and lunging toward Harper.

"Flame, stop it! It's Harper!" The dog promptly sat back down but continued her low growl. I turned my attention to the woman in front of me. "What's going on? Where have you been?" I asked, scanning her for any obvious injuries. There weren't any. In fact, she looked perfectly fine. I frowned. "We've been looking for you everywhere. Are you all right?"

"I'm perfect now that I've found you." Her smile turned to one of pure self-satisfaction, and then magic trickled over my skin, making me chilled to the bone, something that should've been impossible in the summer heat.

It was a spell or a curse, and I was in trouble. My magic flared to life, but before I could do anything to defend myself, Harper disappeared again, and without any other warning, I was stunned with a bolt of electric magic that slammed me against the brick wall behind me. The coffee, water, and pastry bag fell to the ground, the liquid splashing over my sandaled feet. My head hit hard, and my vision blurred as I collapsed to the ground, barely able to hold myself up on all fours. My stomach rolled, and sweat popped out on my forehead as I struggled to hold back the vomit rising in the back of my throat.

Something let out a whimper. It took me a moment to realize the sound was coming from me. Then Flame whined, pressing her little body to my leg. Someone moved above us, and Flame jumped up, barking and growling as smoke puffed from her nose.

"Shut up!" Harper ordered and followed with another blast of cold magic. It hit me right in the chest, and the last thing I remembered before I passed out was Flame breathing a torrent of fire at her mistress.

I WOKE IN A PITCH-BLACK ROOM, the heat so stifling that my dress was sticking to my legs. My head ached, and my mouth was so dry my tongue was practically glued to the top of my mouth. Blinking through the darkness, I pushed myself up from the smooth wooden floor and let out a loud gasp as a shot of pain ran up the side of my abdomen.

"Who's there?" a female voice called from the darkness.

I clutched at my stomach, willing the pain to go away. Silent prayers filled my mind, and I pressed my palm to the side where the pain pulsed.

I see danger for you and your daughter.

Miss Maybelle's words came back to me, and tears filled

my eyes. This was what she'd been talking about. And all I'd been doing was getting cupcakes and coffee. The image of the iced coffee hitting the ground right before I'd been attacked came rushing back. It was like a slow-motion video running over and over in my mind.

"Hello?" the voice called again. "Willa?"

"Willa?" I echoed. "Is she here too?"

"No. I don't... You're not Willa?"

I ran a hand over the back of my head and winced. There was definitely a lump. "No. I saw her earlier today. She was fine. Who are you?"

"Quiet!" a harsh voice called over some sort of speaker. Then the creak of a door reverberated through the room, followed by the unmistakable sound of flesh hitting flesh.

The other woman grunted and let out a low moan.

"Stop it!" I called. "Who's there? What do you want with us?"

There was no reply, just the sound of rustling as I imagined the other woman being dragged from the room.

The door slammed shut, leaving me in the eerie darkness. I had a terrible feeling I'd just been cut off from my only human contact.

"Anyone there?" I tried. Nothing. I wasn't surprised; I hadn't expected anyone to answer. With my head still spinning, I forced my magic to the surface, relieved to feel my powerful magic concentrated in my palms. But instead of trying to blast my way out of the room, I first sent my magic out, confirming that no one else was there.

Except I couldn't release it. It was there, right at the surface of my hands, but when I tried to send it out into the world, it clung to me as if trapped by my own skin. Frustrated, I tried again.

Still nothing.

Then I let out a growl and tossed a bolt of my raw magic toward the area I thought I'd heard the door slam shut. This time my magic flew through the air, but just before impact, it slammed back into me, reverberating through my body and shaking me to my very core.

Another sharp pain ran up the side of my abdomen, causing my knees to weaken from the force. I went down on one knee, still holding on to the wall with one hand.

"Holy hell. That fucking hurt," I muttered, trying to catch my breath and hoping I hadn't cracked a kneecap.

After I got back on my feet, I pressed my hands to the wall and felt my way around the room. There appeared to be nothing but smooth walls, a slightly uneven wooden floor, and two solid wood doors, both of them locked and unmovable. When I tried to use my magic to open the doors, my power rebounded on me just as it had before.

There was no doubt about it. I was in some sort of prison that had been spelled to contain magic. And there was nothing to do but wait.

CHAPTER 17

ime ceased to exist. The blackened room remained silent while my heart seemed to beat in my throat. The pain in my side persisted, intensifying, hurting not only when I moved but when I breathed too. I was no stranger to dangerous situations. I'd fought demons, black magic, evil witches, and vengeful ghosts. A room void of light hardly compared.

But I'd never had a child to protect either. And now I was nearly going out of my mind with fear. I had no way of knowing if I was seriously hurt or if I'd just pulled a muscle. Or when I was likely to be given food or water. Would anyone come back for me? Or was I stuck in this magic-sucking prison forever?

My magic was pulsing through me, charged and on high alert, ready for me to attack at any moment. It was wearing me out. If I didn't control myself, exhaustion would claim me. But I couldn't. My nerves had taken over, and reining myself in was all but impossible.

My frustration and fear swirled around me until I felt as if I'd formed my own tornado, and finally in a fit of rage, I unloaded all my pent-up magic right at the door in front of me.

My magic hit with a boom, rattling the entire structure. The door lit up, illuminating the room's twelve-foot ceilings, an ornate crystal chandelier, one blood-red wall, and the door's deep mahogany color and matching crown molding. The floor was newly refinished, and everything about the room said it was a glorious Victorian except for the bucket in the corner. My modern-day chamber pot, I guessed.

Where the hell was I?

My magic continued to rumble around the room, shaking the chandelier, and then just like that, it winked out as if absorbed by invisible energy. The room went pitch-black again, and suddenly my magic reappeared, slamming back into me.

I let out a cry and slumped to the floor, my energy zapped and the pain now a continuous dull ache in my side. Clutching my abdomen, I hunched over and sobbed, defeated and hating myself for not being stronger for my little girl.

MY REALITY TURNED fuzzy as I slipped in and out of sleep. During my lucid moments, I prayed I'd fall into a deep slumber and that Kane would find me there in my dreams. When I did slip under, my mind whirled with jagged, broken dreams. Women with flaming hands had wolves by their sides with their teeth bared, snarling and ready to battle as they stalked through the bayou in the dead of the night. The blood moon was overhead, and the air was ominous with unease and danger.

Anticipation covered me like a sheen of sweat while I waited… Waited for what, I didn't know. But he was out there, ruling the bayou, making his plans and setting everything into motion.

Jade? His voice was faint but cut through the chaos, soothing my soul.

Kane? Is that you?

Where are you? Are you all right? What happened? His voice was frantic now, his fear creeping into his tone.

Tears threatened to choke me, but I swallowed my own emotion and said, *I don't know where I am. Harper hit me with a Taser or stun gun and knocked me out, and now I'm locked in a room. I think it's a nice Victorian, but I have no idea where.*

Harper? Really?

Yes. She fooled us all. The council was right to arrest her, I said.

Son of a bitch.

He could say that again. I was still standing in the bayou, only the women and wolves were gone, and all I saw was the still water and the sway of the Spanish moss hanging from the cypress trees. *Where are you? Why can't I see you?*

I can't find you. His tone was full of frustration. Then it softened as he asked, *Are you and the baby okay?*

The tears were back, but I'd be damned if I let him hear them or gave him more to worry about. Somehow, I managed to fortify my voice when I said, *We're okay. Ready to go home, but okay.*

Thank the gods, he said, letting out a sigh of relief. *Bea is leading a finding spell tonight, Jade. We're coming for you.*

I don't know if it will work, I said, unable to hide the tremble as I voiced the fear I hadn't wanted to admit to myself. *My magic is contained in this room. I think it's sealed. You might not be able to get a read on me.*

He was silent for a moment. So silent I started to think I'd lost him.

Kane?

I found you in our dreams, Jade. One way or another, Bea and I will find that house. Trust me.

Hope swelled in my heart, and this time the tears flowed freely as I answered, *Hurry.*

THE DOOR banged open and a sliver of light shone into my barren room. I jerked my head up, squinting as I waited for my eyes to adjust. A woman I didn't recognize strolled in wearing a white robe. She dropped a tray on the floor. A bottle of water toppled over and rolled toward the wall.

"Eat," the woman said. Her voice was gruff, and her eyes were almost black against her pale face. She had long, straight gray hair, and her hands were covered with wrinkles and liver spots, but she was agile and moved with ease, defying her aged appearance.

"Where am I?" I choked out.

"Where you need to be."

The door slammed shut, but the lights from the chandelier flickered to life. The light was too bright, causing my eyes to water. I had no sense of time or how long I'd been in that room. Hours? Days? I could no longer tell. I did know I was dehydrated, and the bottle of water looked like heaven. I practically lunged for it, gritting my teeth through the pain in my side.

The bottle was cool in my hand, and I nearly cried tears of joy that quickly turned to frustration as I struggled to open the top. I was weak from the heat and lack of food and water. At least I knew the water wasn't tainted. Leaning against the wall, I sucked in a fortifying breath and twisted. The lid finally moved.

"Thank the gods," I whispered and forced myself to sip the water slowly. Gulping it down would likely only make me sick. After I got half of it down, I eyed the tray of food. It wasn't anything fancy, but it was better than what I'd expected. They'd brought me a chicken sandwich on a croissant, a bag of pretzels, and a packaged brownie. I hadn't had an appetite since I'd found myself in my Victorian prison, but still, for the baby's sake I forced myself to at least eat the sandwich.

Once the sandwich was gone, I tore through the pretzels and the brownie, not leaving a crumb in sight.

The door swung open again, and the gray-haired lady strolled back in. "Good, you're finished. Get up. It's time to find out why you're here."

If there was one thing I wanted besides getting the hell

out of there, it was to know why they wanted me. I hauled myself to my feet, my magic strumming just beneath the surface of my skin, and I followed her out the door. The moment we stepped into the hallway, I pushed my magic out, trying to read her. But just like before, I hit a brick wall and learned nothing.

She chuckled. "You have spunk. I like that about you. But your magic isn't good in this house. You'd be better served conserving your energy."

Dammit. I'd been afraid of that, but I had to try. I shrugged one shoulder but said nothing as I followed her down the stairs and into a large grand ballroom. The house reminded me of the Victorian Kane and I had south of New Orleans. The floor plan appeared to be the same, though the details in Kane's house were more ornate. Not to mention our house was decorated with plenty of gorgeous antiques and artwork.

We made our way through the ballroom and into a formal living room. A broad-shouldered man wearing an expensive suit sat on an ornate love seat with Harper next to him. She was wearing a gorgeous white sheath dress and high heels, and she had her red hair piled up in a fancy updo. Diamonds dripped from her wrists and earlobes.

"Miss Calhoun," the man drawled lazily. "Please, have a seat." He waved to the matching couch that was directly across from the love seat.

Gritting my teeth through the pain in my side, I gingerly lowered myself onto the couch and glared at Harper. She glanced away and visibly flinched. Good. She *should* be uncomfortable, and by the time we were done here, she was going to feel a hundred times worse.

"What am I doing here?"

"I think you know," the man said and took a sip of amber liquid.

"Something to do with leading the dragons?" I asked.

The man looked at Harper. She continued to stare at nothing. He pulled her hand into his lap and exaggerated stroking her skin. "Yes. You're the key to unleashing their full potential. Especially now that you're blessed with motherhood."

I instinctually covered my baby bump with my hands and scowled at him. "Your *girlfriend* over there sent I don't know how many volts into me, knocking me out, while I'm pregnant. Don't think I'm going to help you do anything."

Harper jerked her head in my direction and gasped, "What? I didn't—"

The man squeezed her hand so hard it made her wince. Pure evil rolled off him, and for the first time since I'd walked into the room, I started to think that maybe Harper wasn't one hundred percent on board with whatever was going down in this house. But she had been the one to knock me out, and I wouldn't forget that anytime soon.

The man gave me a cold smile and said, "You'll do what I tell you unless you want to spend the remainder of your pregnancy as my guest."

Cold dread ran through me. Not from his threat that he'd keep me locked up but because he'd been specific about my pregnancy. "Why until then?"

"If you won't work with us, your child will do."

I nearly levitated right off the couch as pure rage fueled my reaction. "You will never take my child," I said, my voice low and full of fury. "If you ever touch her, I will kill you myself."

"Good. I've got your attention." He stood and walked over, holding out his hand. "I'm Zeph Winsor, the man who's going to make you the most powerful woman in New Orleans."

I stared at him defiantly, refusing to take his hand. "I'm already powerful enough."

He pulled his hand back and crossed his arms over his chest, clearly irritated that I wasn't playing his game. "You're in danger. Your *daughter* is in danger."

"The only reason we're in danger is because you've got me in your fun house for... I don't even know what." I met Harper's gaze and stared her down. "How could you do this? Are your missing cousins here too?"

She opened her mouth to speak, but Zeph shot her a look and she promptly closed it, looking away again.

"What is going on?" I demanded, glancing between them. It was clear Zeph was controlling her, but I had no idea if she'd started out a willing participant or if she'd been forced into this arrangement.

Zeph turned to me and said, "There's a war coming. One between the dragons and the council. And you, Jade Calhoun—white witch of New Orleans—are the key."

CHAPTER 18

gain? It was the one and only thought that ran through my mind. I'd been the link between Conor Wells and the dragon soul that possessed him. Was I some sort of dragon magnet or something? Probably.

"And how is that?" I asked.

"You have the power to let the dragons rise." He sat back down and picked up his drink. "And she who unleashes them becomes their leader. I'm offering you the world on a silver platter. I'd think you'd be more grateful."

"Maybe I would be if hadn't been brought here against my will and left in an insufferable, empty room with just a bucket for a chamber pot for God knows how long. Not exactly the most hospitable reception, *Zeph.*" As if I'd ever be grateful to a man who was so obviously an abuser. If it weren't for the fact that the house stifled my magic, I would've blasted his ass into the next room.

"You're feisty," he said with a small, satisfied smile.

Damn that look. It only served to piss me off more. "Are you keeping Harper's family members? Are they here of their own free will? How long until you grab Willa and the others?"

He said nothing, but the various emotions flashing over Harper's face told me everything I needed to know. He did have her cousins, and it was unlikely they'd come along willingly. And the idea of Willa being next was making Harper's body tremble with obvious fury.

"What do you get out of this?" I asked him.

"Isn't it obvious?" He glanced at Harper and took her hand in both of his. "I get this lovely lady and a place at her side."

"He wants my power," Harper spat out, yanking her hand from his.

He threw a ball of magical fire at her, but she was already out of her seat and moving over to me. The fireball winked out and instead burned in his eyes. Flames actually flickered there while his light skin flashed blue, silver, and back again in the blink of an eye.

"You're... Oh. My. God." I gaped at him. "You're already a dragon."

Harper let out a bark of laughter as she sat next to me, her own skin flashing red momentarily. "He has some of the traits, just like I do. But he can't shift, and that's his real goal." She turned to me, disgust in her bright blue eyes. "He wants his wings."

"Who came to who?" he asked. They stared each other down, silent communication passing between them before she glanced away, tears glistening in her eyes.

So she was a willing participant. Or at least she was one to start. Crap on toast. Reading the situation was proving to be impossible.

"Why do you need me?" I asked.

"It should be clear," Zeph said. "Conor Wells. You have the gift."

Only because the dragon soul had been feeding off my magic. I shook my head, refusing to give him an inch. "No. I don't."

His dark eyes glinted. "Oh, but you do." Zeph reached out and grabbed my wrist. His touch burned, the heat crawling up my arm. Tendrils of his energy seemed to seep right into my skin, making me nauseated. Then he tightened his hold, and my magic flowed out of me and into him. The world spun, and horror filled me at what he was doing.

I was being violated, my magic taken against my will, and it was slowly weakening me.

"Stop!" Harper cried. "You'll kill her doing that."

I was certain she was right. My magic was streaming out of me at such a rapid rate that I was having trouble breathing and thinking clearly. Images of Kane flashed in my mind. One showed us holding our little girl, and then one of Kane holding her while they stood near a tomb, tears streaking my husband's face. The day was gray, ominous, and still as a crow flew past him and landed on my final resting place.

"No!" I cried and internally clamped down my magic, even though it did no good. He was too strong. Panicked and having no idea what else to do, I focused on him, concentrating my remaining power and blasting it into his hand where he was still holding me. A crackling noise filled the room as the intensified magic slammed into him and he flew backward, crashing into the nearby wall.

"Run!" Harper ordered. "I'll hold him off."

I didn't hesitate. My choices were to stay and fight, which I could only do if he was touching me, apparently, or try to get out of the house and run for help. I chose to run.

Just as I reached for the doorknob, a familiar, haunting music sounded from upstairs. The violin notes seemed to swirl around me, holding me transfixed in place, and before I knew it, my feet were carrying me toward the stairs, toward the magical music that had possessed me once before.

Liam Colman's music was the only thing that mattered. It filled me up, fortified me, and pulled me right up the stairs and down the hall until I found him sitting on a folding chair in the middle of an empty room, pouring his heart into his violin.

"I knew you would go," Zeph whispered in my ear.

I didn't even jump, though in the back of my mind I knew I should have. I hadn't known he'd followed me up the stairs, hadn't felt him or heard him. Instead, I was completely mesmerized by Liam Colman and his magical violin.

"Don't you understand, Jade?" Zeph said. "You're the key to setting us all free. Me, Harper, her family, and even Liam. Until you help us, we are all bound by the chains of the council."

I glanced over my shoulder at him. His expression was

so earnest, so hopeful—it was an unsettling contrast to the man I'd met downstairs, the one who'd tried to drain my magic for his own resources.

"What is it you expect me to do?" I asked.

"Just help us reclaim our freedom. Let us be who we were meant to be. Dragon shifters who aren't beholden to the angels or the council witches. To be allowed to walk this earth as the universe intended."

The music intensified, and I turned back to Liam, watching as the young man played faster and faster, his music a mix of anger and desperation and longing. The emotions swept over me, cocooning me, and all I wanted in the world was to wrap him in my arms and protect him from his pain.

"Say you'll do it, Jade. Say you'll help us," Zeph whispered. "Say you'll help Liam."

My reaction was immediate. "Yes. I'll help Liam."

The young man in front of me stopped playing and slumped in his chair. As silence filled the room, it was then I noticed his feet and waist were chained to the chair. Exhaustion had set in around his eyes as he collapsed, weak and pale as if he hadn't seen the sun for months.

"Liam?" I said and started to move forward, but Harper let out a cry and rushed past me, flinging her arms around him.

"It's going to be all right now," she said through her tears, kissing his cheeks, his eyes, and his lips. "She's agreed to help. You'll be free soon."

Zeph just threw his head back and laughed. "Free? None of you will be free. You serve me now." He snapped his fingers. Magic burst from him, making me stand at attention.

Fury rose inside me and I grunted, then gasped as the pain in my side intensified. My instinct was to hunch over, but I couldn't. His magic was holding me taut. Just like Liam's... or was it Zeph's magic that had forced me upstairs? I couldn't tell. All I knew was that I was being manipulated by someone's power, and mine was stuck in neutral. Or was it? I had been able to combat Zeph downstairs when he'd been stealing my power.

There was only one way to find out. The magic churning in my veins burst from my palms, heading straight for Zeph. It was powerful enough that it should've obliterated him. Instead, he turned to me, his hands outstretched, and soaked it in, his eyes closed as if my magic had sent him into pure ecstasy.

"Son of a bitch!" I cried and ran toward him, ready to pummel him with my fists if I had to.

But he held his hand out and my feet planted on their own, leaving me frozen in place with no way to fight, magically or physically.

"How are you doing this?" I demanded again. "How are you able to just soak up my magic as if it's nothing?"

"Come, Jade," he ordered. "I'll show you to your new quarters, and then we'll talk."

My feet obeyed without any help from me, and soon I was walking side by side with my captor, his hand on the small of my back. He hummed softly, contentedly, as if he hadn't been imprisoning Liam and me and quite possibly Harper.

"We're going to make quite the power couple, Jade," Zeph said, opening the door to a richly decorated bedroom that was easily four times as big as the one I'd been locked in before. There was a four-poster bed complete with a white silk bedspread and more pillows than Kane and I had in our entire house. The bed looked as though it would feel like sleeping in a cloud. In the space by the window, there was a velvet chaise and two matching antique armchairs, and a gorgeous wood trunk stood at the foot of the bed. Everything about the room was opulent and fit for royalty.

"Our bathroom is through there." He pointed to an open door, steering me into the marble bathroom. I took in the double sinks, a large two-person shower, and a freestanding extra-deep bathtub with bronze fixtures. It was beautiful. And completely terrifying.

"Our?" I finally asked. "You think you and I are going to be a we?"

"Yes." He nodded. "Together we'll be more powerful than the council. My people will walk the earth again, and this time we won't be servants to the angels." He gave me a gentle smile. "Now go clean up." He sniffed the air and wrinkled his nose. "You've gone far too long without a shower."

"Whose fault is that?" I asked hotly, hating the psycho in front of me.

He snorted and pointed, once again forcing my body to act under his will. Once I was inside the giant bathroom, I slammed the door shut and threw the lock.

His amused laughter filtered through the door, and I immediately started searching the cabinets for anything sharp. To my extreme disappointment, there wasn't anything sharper than an unopened eyeliner. I put it on the counter, anticipating its use anyway. A well-placed stab to the throat might be doable.

"Shower!" he yelled through the door. "Now. Then we have work to do."

"Fuck you," I called back and slammed the drawer where I'd found the eye pencil.

"Maybe later."

My entire body stiffened, and if he hadn't been safely on the other side of the door, he'd have suffered a slow and painful death, courtesy of a makeup pencil right through his eyeball. I pretended I hadn't heard him, flipped the water on, and disappeared into the shower where I let my tears run unchecked, purging my frustration and fear. And when I was done, I reemerged, ready to fight with everything I had to save myself and my daughter and get us both the hell out of there.

CHAPTER 19

*W*hen I emerged from the bathroom, I found Harper sitting nervously on the edge of the white bed. She was wearing a blue cotton dress and worrying the hem.

I didn't say anything as I clutched the thick robe tighter and moved to the large armoire, praying there was something, anything, in there that was clean and would fit me. After rummaging around, I found a T-shirt and a pair of sweats and returned to the bathroom to get dressed. When I walked back into the bedroom, Harper still hadn't moved.

"Jade," she whispered, slipping off the bed and moving toward me.

I held my hand up and stared her down. "Don't come any closer. I don't know what's going on with you exactly, but you attacked me with a Taser and you're the reason I'm here. So forgive me if I don't trust you."

Tears filled her big blue eyes, and she shook her head. "It wasn't me. I swear. It wasn't. I'd never..." Her gaze dropped to my belly and grew horrified. "He fucking used a Taser on you... while you're pregnant?"

"He? What are you—?"

"It wasn't me," she said, her voice suddenly earnest "It was Zeph. Don't you understand? He's a witch. A witch with dragon blood. He's behind all this. He's the one who broke me out of the council. He abducted you. He— Oomph!"

She flew backward, landing flat on her back as Zeph stalked into the room, his eyes burning with fire.

"You never learn, do you?" he seethed and mimed picking her up by the neck with his bare fist. Harper rose in the air, her hands clawing at her neck as her eyes bulged. "I told you to keep your fucking trap shut. And what did you do? You went and tried to turn my white witch against me." He jerked his hand, shaking her with such force she swung like a rag doll.

"Stop!" I ran at him, clutching the eye pencil with one hand and aiming straight for his throat. It was a poorly executed, desperate attempt that missed by a mile, but when he jerked out of the way, Harper fell to the ground, gasping for air.

Zeph turned to me, lashed out, and grabbed my wrist, bending it back until I whimpered and the eye pencil fell harmlessly to the floor. He glanced at it, then at me, and shook his head in disgust. "Is that the best you could do?"

"No." I kicked out, connecting with the back of his knee, bringing him down, and then I punched him right in the balls.

He groaned and rolled over, holding himself.

"Let's go!" Harper was back on her feet, yanking me up.

I lumbered upright, glanced at the man writhing on the floor, and hurried out of the room.

Harper pointed me toward the stairs. "Go! I'll be right behind you."

"What?" She darted down the hall and disappeared into the room where I'd last seen Liam.

"You fucking bitch!" Zeph bellowed from the room at the end of the hall. I sped up, hurling myself down the stairs, still ignoring the ache in my side. All I had to do was get outside, get out of this house of horrors, and my magic would be there, waiting for me.

I heard Zeph's heavy footsteps and then Harper's scream as something crashed. But I didn't look back. The door was in my sight, and I lunged for it. The knob wouldn't turn nor would the locks. I let out a cry of frustration but wasn't all that surprised. Zeph had managed to use magic to seal me in a room; there was no reason he hadn't sealed us all in the house. It would make sense, considering he'd given us freedom to roam around.

There was no turning back now. And even though my magic hadn't worked before, I couldn't give in, not when this might be my only chance at freedom.

"Get away from that door," Zeph ordered from the stairs. His voice was low and sinister and crystal clear.

I poured my magic into the doorknob, ignoring him and praying I wouldn't find myself on the hot end of a Taser again. The handle rattled under my grip but didn't budge. Sweat dripped into my eyes, and my body vibrated from the effort, but the door was rumbling under my magic and if I could just—

"Watch out!" Harper's voice sounded from above me.

On pure reflex, I dropped to the floor. A bolt of magic brushed against my arm, searing it before slamming into the door. A loud crack sounded as the door bowed under the pressure.

I glanced back to find Zeph running down the stairs and Harper chasing after him. She had blood running down the side of her face, but her expression was wild, feral-looking, as she let out a wounded sound and launched onto Zeph's back. They rolled down the last five or six stairs with Harper pulling his hair and scratching at his face.

If I was going to get out of there, now was the time. With my magic still sparking at my fingertips, I turned back to the door and spotted a split in the wood. That was it. The split was new, no doubt caused by the blast Zeph had meant for me. I unleashed my magic, finding the weakness that was the crack. With one blast, I managed to create a hole to the outside, breaking through the magical seal.

Warm air rushed in, and I wasted no time reaching through the hole and blasting the lock on the outside knob. The door swung open, and I rushed out.

The blood moon was overhead, shining down on the bayou, the water glinting off to the right. Of course we were way out in the swamp, away from civilization, I thought bitterly. My dreams had been real, showing me enough to know I wouldn't be walking or running into town anytime soon. I glanced around, looking for a vehicle. Nothing.

Dammit.

Another scream came from the house.

No. Not scream. *Screams*. They were coming from the attic. Cries for help.

Harper's cousins? I wasn't sure. But the despair in the air was unmistakable. They needed help. I stood paralyzed in the clearing, torn between walking out of there into the unknown of the bayou in the middle of the night or running back into the house and helping free the women who were locked up.

With the magical seal broken in the house, my powers were fully restored. I could do it. I could beat Zeph. Or at least I thought I could. But if he surprised me the way Harper had back in the French Quarter... I shook my head. That wasn't going to happen this time. I was prepared.

Taking a deep breath, I ran back into the house, finding Harper and Liam both on their knees with Zeph holding a gun to Liam's head. His gaze flickered to me, and a slow, self-satisfied smile broke out over his chiseled face.

"I knew you'd be back." He snapped his fingers, and the cries from above vanished.

"It's a trap, Jade!" Harper cried.

He backhanded her, sending her sprawling to the floor.

Liam reached for her, but Zeph jammed the gun to his forehead.

"Move one more inch and I'll split you in two," Zeph said. "You've already served your purpose."

Liam froze. Harper lifted an arm, her fingers alive with fire, but Zeph stomped on her hand and growled, "Do that one more time and there won't be a warning before I put a bullet in your boyfriend's head."

She went completely still, her eyes wide with fear.

A storm rose inside me, and with only a thought from me, thunder rumbled overhead, shaking the old Victorian so hard the windows rattled.

"Put the gun down, Zeph," I said. "Let's make this a fair fight."

"Nice try, Calhoun." He snorted out a humorless laugh, and without warning, the gun went off. Liam fell to the side, lifeless, blood spilling across the wood floor.

Harper screamed and lunged for Liam, pressing her hands to his chest, trying to stop the bleeding.

Zeph threw his head back and laughed.

I lost every ounce of restraint and let my magic fly. There was no thought, no plan, no spell. It was just raw power that crackled around me. Lightning flashed, the sky opened up, and rain thundered down, the wind howling through the open door.

Zeph lifted his head, seemed to sniff the air, and then snarled as he moved toward me. Magic swirled around me like a vortex, me snuggled inside as if I were safe in my cocoon, his magic bouncing off mine as if he were throwing pebbles instead of fire bolts. Instead of searing me, each time his magic hit mine, the fire winked out, leaving only smoke billowing in its place.

He roared, and a vein popped out on his neck as he stalked forward.

I had my feet planted, my power coursing through me,

unstoppable and full of fury. No one hurt my baby girl and got away with it.

Something glinted in the darkness, and then I heard it. The second shot from the gun that was aimed right at me.

Coward, I thought with venom just as the bullet hit me in the shoulder and sent me plunging into darkness.

CHAPTER 20

$\mathcal{J}$ woke to fiery pain pulsing in my shoulder and something that sounded like weeping. I blinked, trying to clear the blur from my slumber and wondered briefly if I was the one crying. Hadn't I been shot? I reached up and tentatively probed my shoulder. It was wrapped with some sort of makeshift bandage, and while I couldn't see it, I could tell it was dry. At least I wasn't bleeding out. The wound couldn't be that bad, could it?

Banging from down below caught my attention, and I tried to sit up. Red-hot fire burned through my arm, and I cried out, falling back onto the soft surface.

"Jade?" a pitiful voice asked.

"Who's there?" I whispered, feeling around with my good arm and realizing I was on a bed. The mattress was narrow. There was no chance I was in the large bedroom I was supposed to "share" with Zeph. At least I'd managed to escape that horror.

"Willa," she said through a sob. "Where's Harper? Is she here?"

"I think so." But the truth was I had no idea. What had Zeph done with her and Liam after he'd shot me? Had he killed them? Had Liam died from the gunshot wound he'd suffered? Were they chained to a chair again?

"What does that mean?" she asked, the tears so thick I could barely understand her.

I sighed and finally managed to push myself up, but as I moved my legs, I heard and felt the shackles.

Shit!

Zeph wasn't taking any chances that I might get away again. I was certain the banging I heard coming from downstairs meant he was repairing the front door. I'd had my chance to escape and I'd blown it. Sighing, I closed my eyes, willing myself to wake up at home. Willing this all to be a dream.

"Jade?" Willa asked again.

"Yeah?" I was bone tired, mentally and physically. The ache in my side throbbed in time with the wound in my shoulder. But when I put my good hand on my belly, I felt my little girl move, and I let out a sigh of relief. She would be okay. She had to be.

"Where are we?" she asked.

"The bayou," I said, my voice full of exhaustion. "How long have you been here?"

"I don't know," she said. "A few hours maybe? I can't believe I was ever infatuated with that asshole. Can you believe he hit me with a Taser? Then I woke up here, handcuffed to the wall."

My heart sank. Goddamned Tasers. Is that how we'd all been taken out? Then it hit me. She'd said "he." Harper had gotten me. Who had he sent for her?

"Who used a Taser on you? Zeph?"

"Who's Zeph?" she asked, sounding confused. "No. Liam. He showed up at my apartment and said he needed to talk to me. Then he attacked me, and I woke up here."

"A couple of hours ago?" I asked, shaking my head. That was impossible. The man had been shot. I didn't even know if he was alive.

"Yes. Did he hurt Harper too?"

I squinted through the darkness, just making out the outline of her body propped up against the wall. "Willa, it wasn't Liam. I'm sure of it."

"Yes, it was. He said he had news about Harper, and then he..." She went silent.

"Then he what?" I asked.

"He asked what I was listening to, which I thought was really strange since it was his music. A recording of the piece he's been working on for months."

"It wasn't Liam," I said flatly. "Someone's been using illusion spells." I was positive. Harper had tried to tell me she wasn't the one who'd attacked me. And I knew it was impossible that Liam had gone after Willa. If he was alive, he was in pretty bad shape. Zeph was behind all of it. He was a powerful witch with no conscience and a desire for unlimited power. It was the worst combination.

"Then who?"

"Me." The light flickered on with the sound of Zeph's voice. "And you, Willa, are my leverage. Right, Jade? You wouldn't want anything to happen to someone else, would you?"

My eyes narrowed, and I glared at him. He was shirtless, his chest smeared with dried blood, and he had a wild look in his gaze. *Madman* was the word that came to mind.

"What is it you want from me?" I asked, ice dripping from my tone.

"You know what I want. All you need to do is awaken the dragons within and you'll be free to go."

Harper ran past him and clung to Willa, both of them weeping.

I stared at him and in a matter-of-fact tone said, "You're lying."

He shrugged. "Maybe. But you'll do it anyway, otherwise poor Willa over there will join her cousins in the unmarked graves behind the house."

Willa let out a loud gasp, and Harper tried to soothe her, murmuring reassurances.

Ghosts. That's who I'd heard in the attic when I'd been outside. They'd been calling out for help and I'd been too late. "Why did you kill them, Zeph? To siphon their power?"

He shrugged one shoulder, confirming my suspicion.

"Just like you'll do to me once you get what you want?"

His eyes glittered with anticipation, and there was no denying I'd hit a nerve. But then he said, "We still have two months."

My hand tightened over my belly. My child. He wanted her. "It's never going to happen, you slimy piece of—"

"Now, now, Jade. No need to be nasty." He glanced at Willa and Harper then back to me. "You'll do as I say or else you'll be the guest of honor at my private show with Harper's favorite cousin."

"You're a disgusting piece of trash, you know that?" I asked him.

"So I've been told." He walked over and yanked Harper up by her neck. "Time to treat your boyfriend. Don't want him dying while he's still useful." He tossed her across the room, and she landed on her knees with a quiet *oomph*.

He stared at her backside, lust flashing in his normally cold gaze. And I wanted nothing more than to blast his dick off right then and there. Harper got to her feet, and with her head held high, she walked out of the room. Zeph laughed and followed her.

"Jade? Oh goddess. How are we going to get out of this?" Willa asked with a tremble in her voice.

I didn't answer. I didn't have one to give her.

THE STORM RAGED OUTSIDE, rain pelting on the windows, drumming on the roof, and gushing over the sides of the gutters. The force of it was so loud I almost couldn't hear Zeph's demands.

But still his voice cut through the rumbling thunder and the rustling of limbs against the house. "Let it go, Jade. Will your magic to me."

We'd been moved back to the ballroom. My feet were still shackled together, but my arms had been zip-tied to a high-backed velvet armchair. Willa and Harper sat in two identical chairs, the three of us forming a large triangle with

Zeph right in the middle of us. Willa was chained around the middle while Harper was free to move around at will, though if she didn't obey Zeph's every order, he threatened to end Liam's life for good.

The musician was lying on the floor at Zeph's feet, blood soaking his chest. He was barely conscious, his breathing shallow and his skin so pale he looked like death had already taken him.

"The sooner you give me what I want, the sooner this nightmare will end for all of us. Don't you want to be a gracious guest, Jade?" he said conversationally, as if I'd walked in and asked for this bullshit.

What he wanted was my magic. He wanted to steal it, build his power, and then I suspected he'd steal Harper's and Willa's too once their dragon powers had been unleashed. We'd be used up and cast aside while he went on to wreak havoc and destruction through New Orleans. I understood what he wanted, but I didn't understand his reasons.

"Why?" I asked him, not bothering to hide my defiance. "What happened to you that you're so determined to steal our power?"

His eyes flashed with fire, the flames licking at his pupils. "That's none of your business."

"Oh, I think it is," I spat out. "You want me to willingly give you my power. Don't I at least deserve to know why you need it so badly?"

"I could just take it from you," he said.

"You could. But since you aren't, I'm guessing there's a reason you need me to give you my magic of my own free will. I'm not going to until you tell me the truth." My words were full of bravado I didn't actually possess. I knew that in the end, if it meant saving my daughter or saving myself, I'd do what I had to in order to keep her safe even if it meant succumbing to his barbaric demands. But I had to try.

He chuckled. "Nice try, Calhoun. We both know you're outmaneuvered here." He glanced down at Liam then at Willa and Harper. "I bet you wouldn't like to see your friends suffer." Without any other warning, he stomped down on Liam's shoulder, making the violinist nearly levitate right off the floor as he screamed in pain.

I glanced away while Harper flung a string of obscenities at Zeph. They weren't my friends exactly, but that didn't mean I could stomach watching them suffer.

"What happened to you?" I tried again. "Were you born with a black soul?"

He stared flatly at me.

"No mother to love you? An abusive father?"

Still silence other than the storm raging outside.

"What is it, Zeph? Did your first girlfriend rip your heart out and shred it, and now you need to prove to the world just how much you *matter?*"

"Shut up," he said. "That's enough."

"Ah, so that's it. You were scorned by a woman. What did she do to you? Cheat? Drop you for someone more powerful?"

"Delphinia did not drop me for—"

"Delphinia!" I cried. "She was your *girlfriend?*"

His face turned so red it verged on purple. "Give me your magic!"

Delphinia was the witch who had been at the center of trying to unleash the dragon soul that had infected Conor Wells just two months ago. If Zeph was in love with her, his obsession with dragons suddenly made all the sense in the world. "So, you thought that if you became a dragon you'd get Delphinia back, is that it? You know she's locked away for her crimes, right?"

"Of course I know," he spat out. "But when I possess your power and that of the dragon, no one will be able to stop me. Delphinia and I will show everyone what this world can really be. We'll unleash her ancestor together and rule over the witches, the angels, and eliminate the demons altogether. Think about what this world can really be like. No more angel-demon wars. No more black magic. With the dragons as protectors, the world will be safe again, free of evil and pain."

He was a madman. Delusional in the extreme. "You mean free of people like you?" I asked with a humorless laugh. "You'll never eradicate all evil. Especially when it clearly lives inside you."

"I'm a product of the world I live in. Now give me your magic!" He lunged for me. I clamped down hard on my magic, shielding it just like I did my empath abilities when I didn't want others' emotions overwhelming me. My imaginary glass silo went up around me and I held steady, unwilling to give him what he wanted.

His hand wrapped around my throat, and he leaned in so close I could smell the whiskey on his breath. "You will willingly give me your power, or I will choke the life out of you, save your child, and raise her as my own. When she trusts me, she'll give me her power and I'll free Delphinia. The two of us will rule with your daughter as ours."

Pure, unadulterated rage welled up inside me, and I wanted nothing more than to blast him with my magic, but I instinctively understood what he was trying to do. If I used my magic on him now, he'd only take it for himself, wear me down, and then try to coerce me again.

It was a no-win situation, leaving me with no outlet for my magic-filled fury. All I could do was open my mouth and scream.

The lights flickered on and off. Zeph knelt in front of me, smirking with satisfaction, unaware of what was happening behind him. Liam had finally sat up, his pale face lined with hatred as he lunged forward and tackled Zeph. The two went down in a tangle of arms and legs, and before anyone could make sense of the fight, a gun went off and Zeph stilled, his blood seeping into the floorboards.

The lights came on. Liam's eyes rolled into the back of his head, and he passed out right next to his tormentor. Harper, Willa, and I sat in silent shock for just a moment before the door burst open and the cavalry arrived.

CHAPTER 21

*K*ane rushed into the house, Lucien and Bea right behind him. "Jade!" he called, brandishing his dagger, ready for a fight.

"I'm here," I said weakly, slumping over in the chair.

He wasted no time cutting off the zip ties, but when it came to my shackles, he swore. "Dammit. Bea?"

My mentor was hovering over Liam, her magic glowing as she went to work on his wounds. "I'm a little busy, Kane," she said, out of breath.

"I've got this." Lucien stepped in, pressing his hands to the shackles. Sweat poured down his face as he struggled to magically free me from the restraints. "Jade, can you lend a hand?"

I pressed my palm to his arm, sending a bolt of my pent-up magic straight through him. His hands lit up like a firecracker show, and just like that, the restraints disappeared.

"Son of a… That was more than I was bargaining for." He peered up at me. "Oh my god, Jade. What happened to your shoulder?"

"I was shot."

"That bastard fucking shot you?" Unadulterated rage streamed off Kane. He was vibrating with it.

"It's just a flesh wound," I said weakly, suddenly trembling with shock. *Just a flesh wound?* Was I sure? It had to be, otherwise I would've already bled out.

Kane rolled his shoulders, visibly trying to calm himself. "You're going to be all right now, love. I've got you. Understand?"

I nodded, but tears rolled down my cheeks, all my fear finally getting the better of me. In the next moment, I was in Kane's arms and he was holding me tight as I shook with sobs.

"It's all right now, love. You're safe. You and the baby. You're both going to be fine now."

"I've… my side… it hurts," I choked out. "Need to see Healer Hanna."

"An ambulance is on its way, love." He glanced at Lucien, his eyes wild. "Right?"

My covenmate nodded. "Yes. As soon as we knew this was the house, I called. They'll be here shortly." Lucien quickly moved over to Willa, working on getting her free from her restraints.

"You felt my energy?" I asked Kane.

He nodded. "Bea did a finding spell. We knew you were somewhere in this general area. The storm has your energy signature all over it. But the rain is so heavy and the storm so enormous, it took us a while to find this place. We've been trying to penetrate the house for over an hour." He glanced at Zeph, who was still lying unmoving on the floor. "Who shot him?"

"Liam."

Bea and Harper were furiously working on saving the young man, and a lump formed in my throat.

"I thought he was behind all this, and it turns out he's the one who saved us all."

It wasn't long before the sound of sirens filled the air. The paramedics rushed in and whisked Liam away, Harper never leaving his side. Lucien stayed with Willa, making sure she didn't break down. And Kane carried me out while the paramedics did their duty, checking on Zeph.

There was only one ambulance, and Liam was the priority. Kane cursed and started to move toward his car, which was parked behind Lucien's Jeep. But then a bolt of magic came out of nowhere, hitting him in the back, and he stumbled forward, nearly dropping me in the swampy mud.

Bea let out a cry, also caught off guard with a bolt of fire hitting her right in the chest. The flames took over as she quickly wielded a spell to fight the magic.

Kane put me down and turned to face our challenger.

It was Zeph. He was standing on the front porch, fire licking his hands. "You're not taking her anywhere," he roared and then jumped, leaping through the air with impressive height. He landed right in front of Kane and threw a powerful punch that knocked him back two feet, hard enough to dent the Lexus.

"Kane!" a voice called, and Pyper appeared. She'd been in the Lexus, waiting for us.

I threw my good arm out, raw power streaming from me, but instead of Zeph being knocked back, he opened his arms wide and accepted my power just as he had before. Dammit. I'd hoped that leaving the house meant his connection to my magic had been broken. It wasn't. I quickly switched gears and concentrated on a fallen limb. My magic was so charged all it took was a flick of my wrist and the limb went barreling toward him.

He ducked and let out a laugh as he took a step toward me.

"Get away from her, you fuckstain," Pyper spat out, jumping in front of me.

"Pyper, no!" I cried.

Zeph's fire magic came right at us.

I grabbed her and pulled her down. We both slid into the mud, getting coated from head to toe as the car behind us went up in flames.

The scene was complete chaos as Kane got back onto his feet, his dagger in hand. Together with Bea and Lucien, the three of them encircled Zeph, closing in on him as he sprayed fire bomb after fire bomb at them. Mini bonfires popped up all around him, making it impossible for Kane, Bea, or Lucien to penetrate his field. The fire grew and started to spread out, tendrils of fire aiming right for each of them. No matter where they moved or what they did, the fire kept coming.

Bea was doing everything she could to direct water from

the bayou to put the fire out, but it didn't work. It was magical. Nothing could squelch it.

Finally, Bea dropped to her knees, raised her hands to the sky, and started to chant. Lucien followed suit, and even though I had no idea what or who she was calling, I did the same while Kane used the jewel in his dagger to slowly push the fire back to keep the three of them unharmed. But it was a losing battle. The moment he pushed one stream back, more came at them. He couldn't keep it up for forever.

I kept my eyes on them as I chanted an unfamiliar Latin phrase.

Pyper was yelling something, but I couldn't make it out.

Then she grabbed my hand and shook it, pointing just off to the right.

My eyes widened as I spotted the giant fourteen-foot alligator we'd met at Elijah's place. The gator was moving quickly, his muscular tail flicking back and forth, propelling him forward straight toward Zeph. The fire intensified, but it didn't stop the gator. Instead, he sped up and leaped right into the fire.

A loud cry echoed over the storm as the fire rose, turning a light shade of blue and then winking out, leaving the gator sitting in the middle of a burned area, Zeph lifeless next to him.

The storm that had been raging up until then stopped, and Elijah emerged from the trees, two small dogs following him. He walked right up to the gator, patted the reptile's head, and said, "Well done, Trevor."

The gator closed his eyes, clearly reveling in the

attention, and rested his head on Zeph as if showing off his prey.

"Is he really dead this time?" Kane asked, still holding his dagger, ready for any sudden movements.

"I'd say so." Elijah crouched down and studied the body. "Looks like Trevor severed the carotid artery." He pressed two fingers to the other side of Zeph's neck. "Definitely dead."

Bea stood over the body and nodded. Then she raised her arms, closed her eyes, and called, "Goddess of the dead, take this man's dark soul. Remove it, destroy it, purify the body, and let him never rise from the ashes."

The wind picked up, rushing past her, making her auburn hair fly back. She was radiant in the darkened night, light illuminating her hands as she pressed them to the body.

A faint light in the shape of a shadowy figure emerged and covered Bea's hands with her own. The light seeped into Zeph, lit him up like a Christmas star, and then rushed into the goddess. She emerged from the dark, glorious with her long white hair, brilliant amber eyes, and golden sun-kissed skin. She smiled down at Bea, thanked her for the gift, and vanished into the night, leaving only a pile of ash where Zeph used to be.

We all stood by silently, waiting for the other shoe to drop. When nothing happened, Kane strode over to me and wrapped his arms around me, his relief and love wrapping me in a cocoon of his emotion.

"Are you okay, love?" he whispered in my ear.

I clung to him. "I think so. Are you?"

"Perfect now that you're back in my arms." His hold tightened around me, and even though I was covered from head to toe in mud, I thought he might never let me go.

"Jade?" Pyper asked, pressing her hand to my back.

I pulled away from Kane but didn't let go. "Yes?"

She frowned as she stared up at the large Victorian. "Is there anyone else in the house?"

I glanced around, spotted Willa with Lucien and Harper climbing into the ambulance where they'd taken Liam. "I don't think so. Why?"

Her brow furrowed. "I hear something."

Kane stiffened as she moved toward the house. "Pyper, no. Don't go in there. Not until it's been searched."

"I have to," she said, her voice sounding ethereal. "They're calling to me."

Bea strode over to her, took her by the arm, and said, "I'm going with her."

"So am I," Kane said, but as the words left his lips, he glanced down at me, clearly struggling with leaving my side.

"No," I said softly. "I don't think they need you." I tilted my head up and eyed the window in the attic. "Pyper's got this one."

He frowned, and then recognition dawned in his gaze. "Ghosts?"

"I think so. Previous victims."

"Dammit," he muttered, shaking his head.

"There was nothing we could do. I think they were gone before I even got here." Exhaustion washed over me, and my head started to spin. I clutched at him and said, "I think I need to sit down."

"Of course." He tucked me into the back seat of the Lexus and then turned to shake hands with Elijah.

The man clapped Kane on the back. "You were impressive, my man. If you ever need backup again, you know where to find me."

Kane glanced at the alligator sitting at Elijah's side. "That's one hell of a familiar you have there."

Elijah laughed. "That he is." The man knelt down, said something the two pups that had followed him, and then pointed to Willa and the ambulance. The two schnauzers bounded away, one jumping into the ambulance and the other hurling itself at Willa.

"Elijah," I called, watching Willa's pup plant kisses all over the girl's face.

"Yes, Jade?"

"Do you have any idea why Flame—err, Peanut—kept coming to my house while Harper was missing?" I asked, genuinely confused. "Why didn't she just go back to you or stay with Willa?"

He gave me a patient smile. "Because, my dear. Familiars do their masters' bidding. If Peanut kept coming back to you, it's because Harper ordered her to. I'm guessing Harper thought you were her best chance of surviving this nightmare. With her familiar around, you weren't likely to give up on her."

"I wouldn't have anyway," I said, knowing that to be the truth. I'd never been able to walk away when someone was in trouble. Clearly that was never going to change.

He reached through the window of the car and squeezed my hand. "Then you're a rare one, Ms. Calhoun, and Harper was smart for putting her faith in you. Just don't give up on her now."

"What do you mean?" I asked, cocking my head to the side.

He glanced at Willa and the ambulance leaving the clearing. "She's going to need your influence with the council. I fear she's stepped out of one nightmare only to end up in the middle of another one."

Crap on toast. He was right. The council would never let dragons roam free. The fact that Harper and her cousins all had dragon traits put them in danger of being eradicated. Would the council lock up their souls too? The idea was so disturbing that my stomach turned.

I stared him in the eye and said, "I'll do whatever I can. That's a promise."

He mimed tipping his hat, shook Kane's hand, and then with Trevor by his side, he disappeared back into the bayou.

"How did you hook up with him?" I asked Kane.

He opened the back door and sat next to me while we waited for Pyper and Bea. "We found him while looking for you. When he heard you were somewhere in the bayou, he offered to act as a guide of sorts. Brought us straight here when I described what you told me. Strange fellow with his alligator familiar. It's interesting that the two dragon familiars ended up back with him when you and Willa both went missing."

"Yeah, interesting," I agreed. But as I watched the area where Elijah had disappeared, I had a feeling that Elijah had found my search party, not the other way around. I strongly suspected that Elijah was a seer of sorts and knew almost everything that went on in the bayou. If that was the case, then he'd probably been waiting for someone powerful enough to help him bring Zeph down. Good. It never hurt to have friends in the most unexpected places.

The front door of the Victorian swung open. Bea and Pyper emerged with Bea holding Pyper tight, keeping her steady. My friend's face was colorless, and she looked like she was going to throw up.

"Pyper?" I called, ready to climb out of the car. "What is it?" I met Bea's gaze. "Is she all right? What happened?"

"I…" Tears rolled down Pyper's cheeks as she shook her head. "He's a monster."

"They're free now," Bea said gently and pulled her in closer with a sideways hug. "You freed them. They won't have to live that nightmare ever again."

"His victims," I whispered. "They were trapped in the attic."

"And reliving their deaths over and over again!" Pyper yelled, fury streaming off her. "If he wasn't already ash, I'd burn his worthless human shell."

"So would I, dear," Bea said with venom. "But we've already obliterated him. He can't hurt anyone anymore."

Pyper trudged through the mud and without saying another word, she climbed into the front passenger seat.

I reached between the seats and squeezed her shoulder. "You did a good thing, Pyper."

She bowed her head and silently wept.

I leaned back, pressed a hand to the side of my abdomen, and said, "Kane. Take me to Healer Hanna."

He glanced at me, worry in his dark gaze. "You're not okay, are you?"

"I'm... I don't know. I've had a pain in my side. I think the baby is fine, but—"

Kane jumped into the front seat, cranked the engine, and waved at Bea and Lucien as he peeled out of the clearing, spraying mud with his back tires.

CHAPTER 22

*T*he steady *beep, beep, beep* of the monitor was a familiar sound. It seemed that ever since I'd moved to New Orleans, hospital stays had become somewhat commonplace. But I welcomed the sound, relieved that our daughter was fine. Zeph hadn't managed to hurt her. But because of the stress and trauma I'd endured, I'd started to go into premature labor. As a result, I was on a prescription of special herbs and bed rest. The pain in my side had indeed just been a pulled muscle. And I'd been right; the bullet hadn't hit anything vital. My wound was already sealed thanks to Healer Hanna, who said I was one hell of a lucky witch.

I had to agree.

The door swung open, and Kane walked in. "Morning, beautiful."

Smiling up at him, I patted the edge of my bed. "I missed you."

He chuckled and placed a cup from the Grind on my side table. "I was only gone for forty-five minutes."

"I know, but it's lonely in here." I exaggerated my pout. I'd been in the hospital for three days already and was going out of my mind with boredom. "Please tell me you're taking me home today."

He sat next to me and handed me a bag. "I am if Healer Hanna signs off."

I opened the bag and breathed in the vanilla-and-cinnamon scent. "Oh man. Tell Pyper she's my favorite and I'll love her for forever."

"Never. You're mine." He leaned down and brushed his lips over my forehead. I knew he meant the words to be light and playful, but they came out gruff with a side of caveman. He wrapped his fingers around mine and squeezed. "Do you know how hard it was to leave you just to get breakfast?"

Of course I did. Kane had barely been ten feet from me since he'd carried me into the hospital three days ago. He'd slept by my side, carried me to the bathroom, helped me shower, and in general tended to my every need. "Kane?"

"Yes, shortcake?" He brought my hand up and pressed his lips to my knuckles.

"You do realize that if you keep this up for two months, I might have to hex you, right?" I gave him a sweet smile to lessen the blow.

He raised one eyebrow, taking my criticism in stride. "Are you saying you're tired of my hovering?"

"Not exactly. But once I get out of here, I'm pretty sure I will be. It's not that I don't appreciate it. I do. It's just—"

"I know." He pressed a hand to my belly and stared down at me, his dark eyes soft and vulnerable. "You have no idea what it was like for me when you went missing. When we found the spot where you'd dropped Bea's latte and the bag of pastries, I could feel your fear concentrated there. And I thought…"

I squeezed his hand, willing him to finish.

He blew out a breath and shook his head. "Never mind what I thought. But panic settled in my gut, and even though we found you and you're here with me, I still can't shake that feeling. It gripped me from the inside out, and Jade? I'm still reeling from it. Being away from you physically hurts. So forgive me if I'm a little overbearing. Okay?"

"There's nothing to forgive." I reached up and brushed a lock of hair out of his eyes. "Just take me home, love. I want to nest with you and the little one and get ready for the next chapter."

His eyes glinted with tears, but then he blinked and they were gone. "You got it, love. Anything you want."

"I just want you."

He smiled down at me, and we shared a silent moment filled with all the love that was too big for either of us. Finally, he lowered his lips to mine and kissed me softly. Then he handed me the cup from the Grind and said, "Decaf chai latte from Pyper."

I pushed myself up and took a long, fortifying sip. "Okay, I think I love her almost as much as I love you."

He chuckled, positioned himself so he was sitting next to

me, and wrapped an arm around my shoulders. "Good thing I feel the same way, otherwise I might get jealous."

"Nah. I'd just do that thing you like, and you'd forget all about her."

His eyes glinted with mischief. "Don't tease me, Jade. I'm pretty sure the image that just flashed through my mind is off-limits for a few months."

I sighed and patted my abdomen. "Yeah, probably."

"She's worth it," he whispered.

"I love you."

He pressed his lips to my temple and said, "Ditto."

BY MIDMORNING, Healer Hanna had me discharged and set a follow-up appointment for a few weeks later. My bag was packed, I was dressed for the first time in days, and I was more than a little impatient to get going.

"I'm ready," I said, clutching my overnight bag.

Kane handed the clipboard to the discharge nurse and turned back to me. "Okay. Let's roll."

"Finally." I leaned back in the chair, and even though I was dying to walk out on my own two feet, I tried to relax as he pushed my wheelchair down the stark white hall. But instead of heading toward the exit, Kane steered the chair in the opposite direction and took me up to the ICU so we could finally see Liam.

Harper was waiting for us just outside his door. Her eyes filled with tears when she saw me, and before either of us said a word, she wrapped her arms around me and gave me a gentle hug. When she released me, she asked, "How are you doing?"

"Better." I grabbed her hand and squeezed it lightly. "My healer just wants me to rest, keep everything low-key until the baby gets here."

"I'm sorry, Jade," she said, trying to blink back tears. "I should've never dragged you into this."

I sat up straighter. "What do you mean, drag me into it? Wasn't it pure chance that Pyper and I were in the store when you were hauled away by the council?"

"Yes, but..." She squeezed her eyes shut, looking pained. "It was me who told the council that you were the key to sorting this out. If I hadn't left Peanut with you or said anything to them, they probably wouldn't have ordered you to find me."

I shook my head. "I doubt that. Pyper and I were already looking into what happened. It was because of the dragon thing. It's likely I would've been in the middle of it anyway."

Kane snorted but kept his comments to himself.

"Let's not play the blame game, okay? It's not your fault Zeph was an insane black-magic user who was willing to do anything to get what he wanted."

She glanced down and nodded. "Thank you for that."

"How's Liam?" I asked.

"He's... okay. Getting better." Frowning, she glanced back at his room. "Do you want to see him?"

"If he's up to it." I wanted to thank him for being so brave and saving us all. If it hadn't been for him shooting Zeph, who knew what would've happened?

"Let me check." She disappeared into the room for a

moment, and when she returned, she waved for us to follow her in.

Liam was propped up on a couple of pillows, his arm in a sling. He had a fading black eye and a splint on his left knee, and who knew what other injuries he'd suffered that we couldn't see. He hadn't fared very well at all through the ordeal.

"Hi," I said and held my hand out. "I'm Jade Calhoun."

He lifted his good arm and shook my hand, his grip surprisingly strong considering his current state. "Hello."

"This is my husband, Kane Rouquette."

Kane nodded at the young man and said, "Thank you, Liam. I believe I owe you my deepest gratitude. I understand if it wasn't for you, we'd have had a much harder time getting in to help you guys."

Liam just blinked at us. Then he shook his head. "I don't remember anything."

"You shot Zeph, Li," Harper said gently. "He was trying to force Jade to give him her magic so that he could—"

"I know," he said, cutting her off. "You told me. I still don't remember it."

I glanced at Harper and then at Kane. "Do you two mind if I have a moment alone with Liam?"

"Sure, babe." Kane kissed me on the top of my head and backed toward the door.

Harper hesitated.

"It's fine, Harper," Liam said. "Go. I'll be okay."

She still didn't move, but when Liam sighed, she got up and followed Kane out the door.

I rolled my chair closer to the side of his bed but didn't say anything. I just let the silence settle between us.

After what seemed like forever, Liam sighed and asked, "What did you want to talk to me about?"

"Anything you want." I gave him a tentative smile. "Or nothing at all. Your choice."

"I'm tired of people asking me how I am."

I glanced over at him, surprised that was his first response. But then I laughed. "Yeah. Me too."

He eyed my belly and asked, "*Are* you okay?"

"Yeah. This chair is just a precaution. Trying to stave off premature labor. You?"

"No." His tone was full of resentment. "I mean, I'll live if that's what you're asking. But I don't know if I'll play again." He cut his gaze to his immobilized arm. "Shattered bone. Won't know what kind of movement I'll have until it heals."

"Damn," I said softly. "I'm really sorry."

"Me too."

"Do you know who Bea Kelton is?" I asked.

He frowned. "Wasn't she one of the ones who busted in after I shot that bastard?"

"Yep. She's also the former coven leader of New Orleans. She's a badass to the nth degree."

"Oh. Okay."

"And she's the one who conjured the goddess who turned Zeph to ash," I said. "I know that's no consolation for losing something so obviously precious, but I thought you should know who ended that bastard."

He stared at the wall, and then in the quietest voice said, "Thanks."

"I heard you play..." I cleared my throat. "You know, I was going to say I heard you play and it was mesmerizing, but now I'm not so sure. Was that you in the music hall that day last week or someone else?"

"I haven't been back to school since the spring." He frowned as he studied me. "You thought you saw me play?"

I nodded and explained how I'd heard his music and then saw the multiple violins playing on stage. "Was it an illusion?"

"Yeah. Zeph made me play for him and then told me no one would ever miss me. That must've been why."

"Damn." The guy had been an evil genius. I'd suspected illusion spells, but I'd thought Liam had been the one casting them. "I'm sorry, Liam."

"Me too." He sucked in a fortifying breath. "Would you do me a favor?"

"Sure." I leaned in, waiting to see what he had to say, and added, "If I can."

"Can you do whatever you can to protect Harper? I know the council is still after her. They've told her she needs to surrender herself by tomorrow morning. The dragon thing..." He swallowed. "It's not her fault, you know. She can't help what she is."

"They did!" I nearly jumped right out of my chair, wanting to storm down to the council offices right then and there. "Those bastards."

His eyes glinted with a determination I hadn't seen before. "So you'll do it? You won't let them lock her up again? You'll keep her safe?"

"I'll do my best," I said. Then I softened my voice as I asked, "You love her, don't you?"

He jerked his head to stare at me. "Of course. I'd do anything for her." Then he gave me a sad smile. "I already have."

I recognized the love shining through his pain and pushed myself to my feet. Taking his hand in mine, I leaned down and gave him the gentlest kiss on his cheek. "Hold on to that love, Liam. What you feel for her, it's rare and important. More important than your talent. More important than all the crap that's going to be thrown your way. Listen to your heart, prioritize each other, and you'll get through anything. And trust me, with your magic and Harper's dragon blood, you'll need it."

"You think we can survive more of this?" he asked, staring me in the eye.

"You can, and you will," I said, sitting back down. "Trouble finds the powerful, my friend. And you and Harper, you both have special gifts that will call to those who seek to manipulate power. But here's the good news. Together, you're stronger. Hold on to that and just take life as it comes."

He eyed me and then glanced toward the door. "Your husband... Kane?"

"Yes?"

"Does he have magic?"

"Yeah, he does," I said. "He's a demon hunter. We've... seen a lot."

He let out a low whistle.

"But we've also helped a lot of people. It's not always like this." I almost laughed. No, it wasn't always this bad, but it was bad enough. Still, the young couple possessed power others would seek. It was better he be prepared for what was to come.

"Yeah. I can see that." He held his hand out again, and I placed mine in his. "Thank you, Jade. Your visit helped." His words warmed my heart.

"You're very welcome. Now I'll take care of Harper while you concentrate on healing."

"Just make sure she's the one waiting to take me home."

I grinned at him. "It's a deal."

CHAPTER 23

"*I* have to go," I insisted as I got dressed.

Kane sat on the edge of the bed, scowling at me. "Jade, you're supposed to be on bed rest."

Guilt made me wince, and I pressed my hand to my belly. He was right. There was no arguing with him. But I had to get to the council and make sure they didn't do anything stupid like strip Harper's soul from her. "Kane, what else am I supposed to do? You know I won't be able to live with myself if I don't stand up for Harper. You know how the council is."

He sighed and closed his eyes. "This is why we never have a moment's peace."

I sat down next to him and slid my hand into his. "Come with me?"

"Yeah, all right. But if at any moment you feel a contraction or weird pain or even mild nausea, I'm bringing you straight home. Got it?"

"Got it." I smiled up at him.

"Don't do that." He gave me a stern look. "Promise me you won't take any chances."

I drew a cross over my heart with my finger and said, "Promise."

"Is Pyper coming?" he asked, running a hand through his thick dark hair.

"Yes, she—"

"I'm here!" Pyper called from the other room. "Ready?"

Kane raised one eyebrow. "Think she brought coffee?"

"Of course I did." Pyper strode into the room, carrying two cups. She handed one to me and one to Kane. "Pastries are in the car. Let's go."

Kane took the cup from me and handed both back to her. Then, before either of us could say a word, he lifted me into his arms and carried me out to the car and set me in the back seat.

I laughed. "You know, I could've walked to the car."

"Maybe. But one of us has to be cautious." He ran around to the other side and climbed into the passenger seat. Then he leaned over and glanced at Pyper, who was standing on the sidewalk. "Come on. Let's go."

Shaking her head, she climbed into the car, handed us our cups, and then chauffeured us to the council grounds.

"You can't be here," the receptionist at the front desk said. "Madam Tempest told me to tell you to make an appointment.

"We're not leaving," I said. "Madam Tempest put me in charge of finding Harper. I did. Now I need to give her a report. And since I'm not supposed to be on my feet, if I go into labor right here in your lobby because you made me wait, you'll have one massive lawsuit on your hands."

The poor receptionist gulped and stammered, "I'll... um, I'll be back."

Pyper chuckled and leaned against the counter. "Nice."

Kane sat in one of the waiting chairs and tapped his foot impatiently.

A few minutes went by before Madam Tempest appeared. She frowned at me. "Bed rest?"

"Healer Hanna's orders. If you want to hear my report, you'll hear it now."

She gave me a flat stare.

I shrugged.

"Come on," she said, clearly annoyed.

I gave her a pleased smile and indicated Pyper should follow me. Kane didn't move. He knew Madam Tempest would only tolerate so much.

We followed her back to the same room where she'd first ordered us to track down Harper.

"Sit," she said.

Pyper and I glanced at each other and took our seats.

"We're bringing Harper and her cousin in momentarily, but I want to hear from you first," Tempest said.

"Fine." I leaned back in the chair. "Harper isn't a danger to anyone. She didn't try to unleash any dragons. That was Zeph. And do you know why?"

Madam Tempest didn't say a word. She just stared me down, waiting for me to continue.

I sighed. The council would never change. "He used to date Delphinia. He was convinced that if he could steal my magic, he could wield enough power to steal their dragon souls and turn into one himself. He was going to free Delphinia and rule at her side. Whatever that means."

"Yes. That's what we've heard." She waved a hand, and a moment later Kinsley walked into the room. "Was that true?" she asked the young woman.

Kinsley nodded. "It's her truth as she sees it."

"It's what Zeph said," I insisted. "I have no reason to think it's not the truth."

"I understand." Tempest got up and left the room.

Pyper and I glanced at each other and then at Kinsley. "What's going on?" I asked the truth seeker.

"She's going to have Harper testify." Kinsley sat at the head of the table and pulled out a yellow legal pad. A pen appeared out of nowhere and she started to write.

The door opened, and Tempest walked back in. Harper followed but her hands were secured with zip ties.

I scowled at Tempest. "Are you kidding me? She's not a criminal. Why are you restraining her like that?"

"It's standard procedure, Ms. Calhoun," Tempest snapped. "I suggest you calm yourself, or we'll be forced to restrain you as well."

"Holy hell," Pyper muttered. "This place is eight different kinds of crazy."

"It's fine," Harper said, keeping her head held high. "If

this is what I need to do to prove I'm not a threat, then this is what I'll do." She met Kinsley's eyes and said, "Be sure to tell her if anything I say isn't one hundred percent honest."

"I will," Kinsley said with a nod.

"Let's start with the day we brought you in for questioning," Tempest said.

Questioning? Who was she kidding? They'd hauled her in and had planned to charge her with endangerment. But I said nothing, waiting to hear what exactly went down that day.

"Well, I was at work," Harper said. "I hadn't been there long. Zeph, the manager, he sought me out at the deli I worked at. Offered me the job, better pay, better hours. I took it, not knowing he was just trying to keep an eye on me. Anyway, the day the council brought me in, Zeph got word, and he's the one who broke me out of here."

"How?" Tempest asked, her eyes narrowed.

"He's really good at illusion spells," Harper said.

"*Was* good," I interjected.

"Right," she agreed. "Was. Anyway, he spelled himself to look like one of the guards, and when he got in to see me, he spelled me to look like another one and we both walked right out of here without anyone saying a word."

Tempest glanced at Kinsley. She nodded. The council witch leaned forward. "And you willingly went with him? You didn't think maybe you'd be in much deeper trouble when we finally caught up with you?"

Harper let out a humorless laugh. "You're assuming I had a choice, Madam Tempest. Zeph didn't ask my opinion. He just spelled me and then ordered me to go. I couldn't have stayed even if I wanted to."

"I see." Tempest scowled. "Then our defenses aren't nearly as strong as we think they are."

Kinsley continued to scribble notes while Harper went through every gory detail of being locked up in Zeph's Victorian. When she got to the part about Zeph impersonating her to attack me, I paid particular attention to Kinsley. And when she nodded that Harper was still telling the whole truth, I relaxed. The college student had proven herself to me over and over again. As far as I was concerned, she deserved a medal for helping take down Zeph.

By the time she was finished, tears were streaming down her face, but her voice was steady when she turned to Tempest and said, "I know you're going to do what you have to do. But I hope you'll consider my offer."

"And what offer is that?" Tempest asked, watching the woman with interest. I wasn't sure if it was just my imagination, but I could've sworn that the council witch was impressed with Harper's spine of steel. I certainly was.

Harper took a deep breath. "Instead of eradicating me and my family just because we have dragon blood, let us come work for the council."

"Work for us?" Tempest asked, raising a curious eyebrow. "Why?"

Harper got a fierce look on her face as she clenched her fists and said, "Because the one thing I want to do with my life is keep others safe from sick fucks like Zeph. I didn't ask for these dragon powers, but since I have them, I want to put them to good use. Hire us as investigators or enforcers or protectors. Whatever it is you think will serve the council best. But let us work for you to bring down those who seek to utilize their powers for evil."

"Whoa," I said under my breath. I hadn't seen that coming, and judging by the look on Tempest's face, she hadn't either.

"That's not the entire truth," Kinsley said, staring at Harper. "There's another reason you want to work for the council, isn't there?"

Suspicion seeped from Tempest as she eyed Harper. "What is it you want from us?"

Harper let out a bark of laughter. "Isn't it obvious?"

It was to me. And apparently to Pyper too since she rolled her eyes.

"You'll have to enlighten me, Ms. Spelling," Tempest said.

"I don't want to be locked up, or purged of my soul, or any other number of things the council might have planned for my cousins and me. We'd just rather work for you, doing some good, instead of against you." She gave Tempest an exasperated look. "Is that so hard to believe?"

Tempest leaned back in her chair, studying Harper with interest. Then she let out the smallest laugh. "No. I guess it isn't." She cut her gaze to Kinsley.

The truth seeker gave her a short nod.

"Good." Tempest nodded. "Pass her the contract."

We all leaned forward, waiting to see what the contract was about.

Harper took it and scanned the page. When she got to the end, her eyes widened with surprise. Then she looked up and frowned at Tempest. "You were already prepared to offer us jobs? Why?"

Tempest shrugged, the most human gesture I'd ever seen her make. "Let's just say the council understands the value of having dragons on staff. I wasn't sure I was going to make the offer, but after speaking with you, I think perhaps we should go ahead with a trial run. Do you have authority to speak for your cousins? The ones who show signs of dragon magic?"

"Yes," Harper said. She pulled out a notarized piece of paper. It had been signed by her cousins, all of them agreeing to let Harper negotiate on their behalves.

"Excellent. Then our contract will work as is. And anyone in your family who develops dragon magic will be required to register and report to the council as an employee. If they don't, they will be subject to disciplinary actions. Dragons are dangerous. That's a fact. But we recognize that this isn't something you asked for and punishing you for events that are out of your control isn't the organization we wish to be." She nodded to the contract. "Sign it and we're done here."

Harper stared at her openmouthed. But when Kinsley handed her the pen, Harper didn't hesitate. She signed the contract with a flourish and grinned as she handed it back to Tempest.

The council witch verified it was signed, handed it to Kinsley, and then turned to me. "Satisfied, Ms. Calhoun?"

I grinned at her. "Very. And pleasantly surprised by this turn of events."

Tempest rose from her seat. "Try to remember this," she

said to me. "We are no longer the same organization we were during Beatrice Kelton's days as the coven leader." She held her hand out to me. "This isn't the first time we've tangled. But I hope our interactions will be less... contentious in the future."

I eyed her hand but didn't take it. "You know, that would be easier to believe if you didn't send your agents to arrest innocent people and then strong-arm them into doing your bidding."

She gave me a curt nod. "You're absolutely correct. I apologize. It won't happen again."

I glanced at Pyper. She shrugged her shoulders and lifted her hands palms up.

"She's being sincere," Kinsley said quietly.

Tempest scowled at her, but I just laughed.

"Okay, fine." I shook Madam Tempest's hand. "To a cooperative future."

"I look forward to working with you, Ms. Calhoun," she said stiffly. "Good luck with your pregnancy." She dropped my hand, nodded to Harper, and then swept out of the room, her head held high with Kinsley right behind her.

Harper glanced from the door to me and asked, "Did that really just happen?"

"It appears so." I stood and opened my arms to her for a hug. When she pulled back, I said, "Congratulations. I think."

She chuckled. "It sure beats being locked in the dungeon."

"Well," Pyper said with a wicked grin. "I think that depends on the dungeon."

Harper laughed while I groaned. "Someone's been hanging out with Ida May too much."

"Who's Ida May?" Harper asked.

"You'll see," I said and led the way out of the room to go let my husband take me home.

CHAPTER 24

"*Y*ou look gorgeous," I said to Kat, smoothing a lock of her hair as I secured her veil in place. She was wearing a sleek, formfitting white mermaid wedding gown that showed off her incredible figure. "Lucien is going to lose his mind."

"He is, isn't he?" she agreed, her eyes glowing with so much happiness I thought my heart would burst with love.

Pyper walked into the bedroom, holding three champagne glasses. She handed one to Kat and another to me. Leaning in, she said, "Jade, yours is sparkling cider."

I sat down on the bed and sighed. "Of course it is."

"Hey, at least you're here!" Kat said, raising her glass to me.

"I'm so sorry I missed the bachelorette party," I said for the tenth time. "You know I wanted to be there."

"Oh my goodness. Remember this?" Kat said to Pyper, making an obscene gesture.

Pyper cracked up. "Can you believe he did that? Those poor women from Tennessee will never be the same again."

"Hello." I waved a hand in front of their faces. "I'm right here, remember? Pregnant woman who had to spend the evening in bed, unable to partake in the festivities."

"Sorry, Jade," Kat said, her eyes still dancing with amusement. "You'll catch the next one. And don't worry, I have a feeling Pyper's will be epic."

"It will be if you're planning it," Pyper said to her.

"You two seem to have… bonded," I said, watching them closely. They were friends, but they'd been closer to me than with each other. Maybe with my sitting out, they'd found a way to better connect.

"That's what happens when you mix tequila, male strippers, and body shots," Kat said.

"Not to mention penis headbands and phallic chocolates," Pyper added.

I chuckled. "Sounds like a perfect night of debauchery."

"You could say that," Pyper said and smoothed her short red cocktail dress. After searching every bridal store within fifty miles, Kat had finally decided to let us choose our own bridesmaid dresses. The only caveat was that they had to be fire-engine red.

Pyper had gone with a formfitting halter top number while I'd chosen a baby doll style that cinched just above my baby bump. I'd thought it was flattering, but Kane had said it was sexy as hell, and I'd all but had to swat his hands away from me after asking him to zip me up. I was still supposed to be on bed rest, but Healer Hanna had given me the go-ahead to attend the wedding as long as I stayed off my feet as much as possible.

"Kat, I have a surprise for you," I said.

"Oh yeah? I hope it's not another fireball. That thing had me practically ripping my clothes off before I even got in the door the other night." She shared another laugh with Pyper, then pointed at her. "This one is dangerous."

"No, that drink is dangerous," Pyper said. "I warned you to be careful."

"You should've warned me it would make my clothes fall off." A shy smile crossed her lips. "But Lucien didn't complain."

"La, la, la, la, la," I said, sticking my fingers in my ears like a twelve-year-old. "TMI. TMI."

Laughter filled the room, and I grinned at them, grateful for my two best friends. While I hadn't been able to make it to the bachelorette party, Kat had postponed her wedding shower, and we'd had it a few days ago at my house where I'd been relegated to the couch. Everything had been beautiful, from the daisy and sunflower floral arrangements to the ornately decorated sixties-themed cookies. And the food. My goodness. Kat had found a neighborhood chef who'd outdone himself with specialty crab cakes, seafood cheesecake, fried green tomatoes, gumbo, and potato salad. The day had been perfect.

And now I was going to watch the person who'd been by my side for over twenty years marry one of the best men I knew. I cleared my throat. "Are you two done yet?"

Kat turned to me, her eyes sparkling. "For now."

"Good. Like I said, I have a surprise for you."

She glanced around the room. "All right. Where is it?"

"Right here, honey," a woman said from the doorway.

Kat's mouth dropped open and she started to tremble a little as she turned around and stared at the short, round woman who'd just walked in. Her red hair was a shade darker than Kat's, but it was the same curly texture, and they shared the same hazel eyes.

"Mom?"

Mrs. Hart opened her arms and said, "I'm here, sweetie."

Kat flew into her mother's arms, hugging her tightly. "I can't believe you made it. I thought..." She sniffed back tears. "Is Dad here too?"

"I am." Mr. Hart, a tall man of six and a half feet, pushed the door open and walked in, grinning. He wrapped his arms around his wife and only child. "We just couldn't miss this day, Kitty Kat."

Kat pulled away, using the back of her hands to dab at her tears. "But I thought you couldn't fly. How did you get here? Did you drive all this way?"

"Oh goodness no," Hildie Hart said. "You know how carsick I get. And then the anxiety kicks in. Ever since menopause hit, I can barely stand driving more than ten miles into town. That was never an option."

"So you flew?" She glanced at her father.

He nodded. "Hope and Marc came over with some herbs. I'm telling you, they were magic. We took a short trip over to the Oregon coast as a trial run. Your mother took those herbs, and she was chill for hours. It was something else. Who knew?"

"The entire hippie population?" Pyper whispered to me.

I swallowed a chuckle and beamed at them. I'd known my mother would have something that could help Hildie. I just hadn't known if she'd be receptive to any of my mother's woo-woo herbs. "I'm so glad you're here, Mrs. Hart."

"Oh, Jade. If it weren't for you and your mom, I don't think I would've been able to watch my baby walk down the aisle. Thank you." She sat down beside me on the bed. "You have no idea how grateful I am."

"I didn't do anything." I hugged her tightly. "You did. You're the one who was brave enough to get on the plane. And now look at you." I pulled back and nodded my appreciation for her sparkling silver mother-of-the-bride dress. "You're gorgeous."

"Thank you, Jade." She kissed me on the cheek. "Having you in our daughter's life is such a blessing." She got up and walked back over to Kat and her husband. After a few moments, Kat's parents left to find their seats.

"Jade," Kat said, the tears flowing again. "I can't believe you did this."

"I didn't do anything." I picked up the handkerchief I'd been planning to hold during the ceremony and handed it to her.

"Yes, you did. You called your mom and asked her to help. And now my parents are here." She sat next to me, exactly where her mother had been a few minutes ago. "Did you know they were coming?"

I just smiled at her.

"You did! You sneak. Thank you. Now the day is perfect."

We hugged, and through our sappy tears we laughed.

And then when Pyper sniffed after being overwhelmed with emotions, we laughed harder.

Finally there was a knock on the door. "Is everyone decent?" Kane asked.

"No, not when I'm around," Pyper joked as she opened the door. "But don't let that stop you."

He eyed her from head to toe and let out a low whistle. "Looking good, Pypes."

"Thanks. You clean up okay too." She winked at us. "Looks like this party is ready to start. I'm going to go check on the bouquets. See you down there."

After she left, Kane walked over to me and held his hand out. "Ready, pretty witch?"

I glanced at Kat. "Are we ready?"

She nodded soberly. "Just because you're not standing at the altar with me doesn't mean you aren't still my matron of honor. You know that right?"

"Matron. That makes me sound so old." I grinned.

"Yeah. Ancient. I mean, we're talking one-foot-in-the-grave territory. It's amazing your uterus still works." She rolled her eyes at me, laughed, and then sobered. "I just meant to say that even though Pyper's been filling in for you the over the past few weeks, no one will ever replace you in here." She pressed her palm to her heart. "You're the sister I never had, and you always know what I need."

Tears filled my eyes, and I didn't bother to blink them back. There was no point. The day was already too emotional, and it was a losing battle. "Just go out there and focus on getting married. Today is all about you and Lucien," I promised. "Don't worry about a thing."

"Famous last words," she said with a soft smile. "As long as angels don't pop in and order me to track someone down, I think we'll be okay."

Kane and I both laughed at that. The first time Kane and I had tried to get married at the plantation house, that was exactly what had happened. The entire event had been postponed until we'd saved Mati from a void world.

"Not going to happen," I said forcefully. "You've already had your wedding snafu with the postponement of the wedding shower. Today is going to be perfect."

She took a deep breath, straightened her shoulders, and followed as Kane led us both out of the room. Just as we reached the end of the hallway, she whispered, "From your lips to the goddess's ears."

The wedding planner handed Kat and me our bouquets. Then I kissed her on the cheek, wished her luck, and let Kane carry me down the stairs and to my seat in the front row with Kat's mom where I watched as she and Lucien vowed to love each other forever without even so much as a peep from the supernatural world.

CHAPTER 25

$\mathcal{I}$t was a few days before Halloween and my energy level was through the roof. Healer Hanna had finally taken me off bed rest the week before, and I'd been like the Tasmanian Devil, cleaning, organizing, and nesting around the house. I'd even managed to get out to lunch with Pyper and Kat a few times.

After almost two months of nothing but the couch and the bed, I'd been starting to feel like the walls were closing in on me. Today all I wanted was a walk outside in the glorious sunshine. And since Kane was still nervous about me walking the streets alone, I called Pyper and told her I needed an escort.

"Hello?" Pyper called as the front door slammed shut. "Where's the mama-to-be?"

"In here," I called from the baby's room. I was busy putting away diapers, onesies, and all the other million things you needed for a tiny human.

Pyper walked in, carrying her customary paper bag and cup from the Grind. "I brought treats."

"I love you," I said and took the decaf chai from her. "Ready to walk?"

"Are you?" She raised one eyebrow as she looked me up and down. "You look like you're ready to pop."

I glanced down at my oversized belly and sighed. "Yeah. I think that bed rest worked too well."

She chuckled. "Well, sit. Let me put your shoes on you."

I glanced down again, unable to see my feet. "I'm not wearing shoes?"

"You're wearing slippers, Jade." She snorted her amusement, disappeared, and returned with my tennis shoes.

"I'm not sure those are going to work," I said, skeptical. "Aren't my feet swollen?"

"We're about to find out." She knelt in front of me, and after putting some muscle into it, she stood up and jerked her thumb toward the door. "There. All set."

"Cool." I could've been wearing plastic bags on my feet and I wouldn't have noticed. My back ached, and I was hoping a walk would work out some of the kinks.

She opened the door for me, and together we made our way down to the river. The skies were a brilliant blue, no clouds anywhere, and the sun was warm on my skin. I stood at the railing on the pier and tilted my head up to the sun, happiness settling in my bones. Everything had been quiet for the past two months. Kat's wedding had been magical. Pyper's was coming up, and life couldn't be better.

If only my back didn't ache so much.

"Come on," I said to her. "Time to move."

"Jade, maybe we—"

Swoosh.

We both stared at the gush of fluid at my feet that stained the brick walkway. I was frozen, in shock, not quite ready. The cup slipped from my hand and the chai splattered over my feet as the cup rolled away.

"Holy hell, Jade. Looks like the walk worked." Pyper pulled her phone out and tapped the screen. "Kane? Meet us on Decatur outside Café Du Monde. It's showtime." She paused. "Yes. We were out taking a walk."

The pain in my back intensified, and I let out a loud moan as my knees nearly buckled.

"Oh, hell. Hurry. I think she's been in back labor for a while." She ended the call and wrapped her arm around my waist. "Come on, Jade. We need to get over to the street. Kane's picking us up."

"Where is he?" I panted.

"The club. He'll probably be at the street before we can even get down these stairs."

The contractions came on hard and fast, making it almost impossible for me to walk. Pyper did manage to get me down the first set of stairs but then pulled out her phone again and called Kane. "New plan. There's a parking lot behind Washington Artillery Park. Meet us there."

"Is he coming?" I asked through gritted teeth.

Before she could answer, Kane's Lexus screeched to a stop right beside us. Kane jumped out, picked me up, and slid me into the back seat, then yelled at Pyper to drive.

She jumped in, and before I knew it, we were tearing out of the parking lot, dodging tourists with precision.

"Hey, shortcake," Kane said, rubbing my shoulders. "Are you all right?"

"I am now," I said, smiling up at him. "Are you ready to meet our daughter?"

"More than you can imagine." He pressed a kiss to my forehead and placed his hand on my belly just as a contraction hit.

I let out a low moan but welcomed the pain. I'd waited for this day for so long. It was worth any amount of pain to hold my daughter in my arms. Or at least that's what I told myself.

By the time we reached the hospital, I was covered in sweat and was certain the baby was on her way out.

What actually happened was I labored for fourteen long hours, most of it in my back. Healer Hanna tried everything from special herbs to more walking, lunges, squatting, and even a warm bath.

By the time midnight rolled around, I was begging for a C-section.

"I just want to hold my daughter," I whined.

Kane wiped my brow with a cool cloth. "It won't be long now, babe. Hanna says you're almost there. It's almost time to start pushing."

"That's what she said hours ago." It wasn't true, but it sure felt like it. Back labor was a bitch.

"Okay, Jade. Let me take one more look," Hanna said.

I lay back against the pillows and closed my eyes, gritting my teeth as another contraction hit.

"Good. Very good, Jade," Hanna said. "This is perfect. Okay, push. Push now."

Kane moved to the field of birth but didn't let go of my hand. I clamped my fingers around his and pushed with everything I had.

My insides felt like they were being ripped right out of me, but all I could think about was seeing my little girl's face for the first time. I already had a picture of her in my mind with a patch of bright red hair, brilliant green eyes, and Kane's nose. She was soft and pink and full of smiles.

"Is that a storm outside?" one of the nurses asked.

"It sure is," Hanna said. "This little girl is making her presence known."

Magic swirled around us, causing the lights to flicker on and off in time with the boom of the thunder and the flickers of lightning, while wind rattled the windows.

All the while, all I saw was her sweet face.

"Push, Jade," Hanna encouraged.

"There she is. Oh my god, Jade," Kane said, tears in his voice. "I see her. She's almost here."

I clutched his hand, floating in almost a dream state as the storm raged outside.

"One more push. There you go," Hanna said.

I nearly came right off the bed as I bore down and pushed with everything I had.

"There she is," Hanna said. "Come here, Dad. You hold her first. There you go."

I peered over my belly, trying to get my first glimpse of our girl.

Kane was there, tears rolling down his cheeks as he

stared down at her. Then he looked up, met my gaze, and said, "She's perfect. Just perfect, love."

"Give her to mama now," Hanna said gently. "It's time to cut the cord."

Kane handed her off to Hanna, who placed her on my belly.

My vision blurred, but not before I noticed the splash of red hair and the perfect, familiar nose. The noise from the storm disappeared, and the lights stopped flickering as my daughter made cooing noises. Kane was right. She was perfect.

THE SUN SHONE through the hospital window, illuminating my daughter's sweet face. It was morning, and I was sitting up in the bed, watching her sleep. Kane was lying beside us, one arm wrapped around my shoulder as he snoozed just as soundly as the baby.

Happiness like I'd never felt filled my heart and radiated out, filling all the empty spaces inside me I hadn't even known existed. For the first time in my life, I felt perfectly content. Like I could live in this moment forever and be completely fulfilled.

I knew it had to be the post-labor endorphins that were affecting me, but I didn't care. It was a moment I'd remember and cherish forever.

"You did it," Kane said softly.

I glanced over at him and smiled into his sleepy chocolate-brown eyes. "We did it."

He gave me a tiny shake of his head. "I did the easy part." His lips twitched. "Many, many times I might add. To my great pleasure."

I chuckled. "Yes, you did."

He reached up and brushed a lock of hair out of my eyes. "She needs a name."

"She does," I agreed. "I was thinking Juliet Eloise would be nice."

"Eloise was my mamaw's name," he said, softly caressing his daughter's head.

"I know how much you loved her." I reached up and pressed my palm to his cheek. His mamaw had been the one and only person in his youth who'd made him feel loved. Before Pyper and I had come along, she'd been the only one who really cared for him. His parents... they had been the selfish type. "We can make it her first name if you prefer."

He gazed at me with so much love in his eyes I thought my heart might burst right out of my chest. "No, love. Juliet Eloise is perfect. Mamaw would approve."

"I wish I could've met her," I said, watching as our daughter opened her eyes and stared up at us.

"She would've loved you just as much as I do, shortcake."

"I hope so."

We were silent as we both gazed in awe at Juliet. Then she opened her mouth and let out a loud cry, letting us know that from that moment on, our lives would never be the same again.

And all I could think was *Thank the gods*.

Kane grinned at me. "She's got quite the lungs on her."

I nodded. "And just think, you told me last month you wanted at least three of these."

"Now I'm thinking four." His eyes flashed with mischief. "Remind me to ask Healer Hanna when we can get started on the next one."

"Good goddess, man. Keep it in your pants," I said with a laugh. "Let me enjoy this one first." But as I gazed up at him, love consumed me. A vision took hold and I saw the two of us in our old age, surrounded by four beautiful children. Two had strawberry blond hair like mine, and two had thick dark hair like his.

"Don't worry, love. I'm not in that big of a hurry," he said, kissing the top of my head.

I leaned into him with a contented sigh and said, "You know, Kane, if you play your cards right, I think we're both going to end up with everything we ever wanted."

He tightened his arm around me and whispered, "I think we probably already have."

DEANNA'S BOOK LIST

Witches of Keating Hollow:
Soul of the Witch
Heart of the Witch
Spirit of the Witch
Dreams of the Witch
Courage of the Witch
Love of the Witch
Power of the Witch
Essence of the Witch
Muse of the Witch
Vision of the Witch
Waking of the Witch
Honor of the Witch
Promise of the Witch
Return of the Witch
Fortune of the Witch

Witches of Befana Bay:
The Witch's Silver Lining

Witches of Christmas Grove:
A Witch For Mr. Holiday
A Witch For Mr. Christmas
A Witch For Mr. Winter
A Witch For Mr. Mistletoe
A Witch For Mr. Frost

Premonition Pointe Novels:
Witching For Grace
Witching For Hope
Witching For Joy
Witching For Clarity
Witching For Moxie
Witching For Kismet

Miss Matched Midlife Dating Agency:
Star-crossed Witch
Honor-bound Witch
Outmatched Witch
Moonstruck Witch

Jade Calhoun Novels:
Haunted on Bourbon Street
Witches of Bourbon Street
Demons of Bourbon Street
Angels of Bourbon Street
Shadows of Bourbon Street

Incubus of Bourbon Street
Bewitched on Bourbon Street
Hexed on Bourbon Street
Dragons of Bourbon Street

Pyper Rayne Novels:
Spirits, Stilettos, and a Silver Bustier
Spirits, Rock Stars, and a Midnight Chocolate Bar
Spirits, Beignets, and a Bayou Biker Gang
Spirits, Diamonds, and a Drive-thru Daiquiri Stand
Spirits, Spells, and Wedding Bells

Ida May Chronicles:
Witched To Death
Witch, Please
Stop Your Witchin'

Crescent City Fae Novels:
Influential Magic
Irresistible Magic
Intoxicating Magic

Last Witch Standing:
Bewitched by Moonlight
Soulless at Sunset
Bloodlust By Midnight
Bitten At Daybreak

Witch Island Brides:
The Wolf's New Year Bride

The Vampire's Last Dance
The Warlock's Enchanted Kiss
The Shifter's First Bite

Destiny Novels:
Defining Destiny
Accepting Fate

Wolves of the Rising Sun:
Jace
Aiden
Luc
Craved
Silas
Darien
Wren

Black Bear Outlaws:
Cyrus
Chase
Cole

Bayou Springs Alien Mail Order Brides:
Zeke
Gunn
Echo

ABOUT THE AUTHOR

New York Times and USA Today bestselling author, Deanna Chase, is a native Californian, transplanted to the slower paced lifestyle of southeastern Louisiana. When she isn't writing, she is often goofing off with her husband in New Orleans or playing with her two shih tzu dogs. For more information and updates on newest releases visit her website at deannachase.com.

www.ingramcontent.com/pod-product-compliance
Lightning Source LLC
Chambersburg PA
CBHW030330200626
46816CB00006BA/2002